Secret Lives

Secret Lives

~~~~~~~~~~~~~~~~~~~~~

by

Berthe Amoss

A Yearling Book

Published by
Dell Publishing Co., Inc.
1 Dag Hammarskjold Plaza
New York, New York 10017

Yearling ® TM 913705, Dell Publishing Co., Inc.

ISBN: 0-440-47904-5

Reprinted by arrangement with Little, Brown and Company, Inc.
Printed in the United States of America

First Yearling printing—November 1981

CW

For Harriet

Secret Lives

CHAPTER I

M Y MOTHER IS SIXTEEN in her portrait. Only four years older than I am now. Her portrait dress is painted so carefully you can see little waves in the white silk, and threads in the scooped-out lace collar. A gold heart hangs from a chain around her neck, and her curls, almost as golden as the heart, are tied back with a velvet ribbon. Her smile makes you wonder if someone she loved was standing to the left of the painter.

In one hand, she is holding a prayer book with a mother-of-pearl cover; the other hand rests on Fifi, her little white dog. Fifi is looking straight out of the portrait, so real and cute I wouldn't be surprised to see her tail wag. There they sit, the two of them, absolutely perfect forever, on a creamy white sofa, the very one I'm sitting on. Only now, the sofa is covered in scratchy mohair, worn and old like everything else in this house.

It just seems to me that, this being 1937, there ought to be a hint of modern times around here, but Three Twenty Audubon Street and its occupants have been lifted straight out of the Dark Ages and placed in the middle of New Orleans. Not that I'm ungrateful for all of the things Aunt Eveline and Aunt Kate do for me, especially Aunt Eveline, but if it hadn't been for the tidal wave, I wouldn't find myself in a practically haunted house being raised by two old ladies dressed in lavender, who think more about dying than living.

Aunt Eveline had closed the shutters at noon to keep the September heat out, but now the sun was low and bright stripes slanted into the gloomy room across my feet to Aunt Kate, fast asleep in her chair. In a little while Aunt Eveline would bring Aunt Kate her coffee, and Sandra Lee would prance in to hear her favorite radio program. I opened my drawing pad. There was just enough time to copy my mother's portrait dress for Jane Whitmore.

I held my pencil and studied the portrait.

I must have been swapped in the hospital. I don't look anything like my mother. I wonder if I'm adopted and Aunt Eveline doesn't want to tell me for fear it will warp my personality. That can't be it. Aunt Eveline has never even heard of personality.

"Posture is most important, dear," she says. "*Most* important. Hold yourself straight!"

If only I could let go! Nature is holding me — my hair, my nose, and my figure — in absolute, perfect straightness. I could double for a telephone pole. That

4

doesn't bother Aunt Eveline. It's character that counts with her. "Turn the other cheek, dear," she says. She means to Sandra Lee, of course.

Unfortunately, Sandra Lee does look like my mother's portrait, even though she is only my cousin. Same yellow curls and cute turned-up nose, and the beginnings of a real figure. The resemblance stops there. The real Sandra Lee, under all the fakiness, is meaner than sin, and my mother, Aunt Eveline says, was as good as she was beautiful.

I sighed and drew the scooped-out lace collar. I made the skirt wide, with a hoop, and started cutting out. If my mother were here, I might be downtown with her this very minute. Instead of sitting on scratchy mohair making a paper-doll dress, I might be shopping for a dress of my own to wear Friday nights.

"If only you were here," I whispered to the girl in the portrait.

"Darling Pasie!" Aunt Eveline cried out, so loud I almost stabbed myself with the scissors. She was standing right next to me, looking at the portrait, Aunt Kate's special cup in her hand. "Oh, Addie," she said, "if only your darling mother were —"

"Darn!" I interrupted. She'd made me cut a tab off Jane Whitmore's dress.

"Never say darn if you mean damn, and never say damn if you're a lady, dear," Aunt Eveline said, proving how up-to-date she is on bringing up girls in 1937. "I thought you'd outgrown paper dolls." Aunt Eveline doesn't like Jane Whitmore's curves and skimpy underwear.

"I have outgrown paper dolls, but I'm going to be a fashion illustrator someday and I'm practicing." It was almost the truth. I am going to be an artist but I don't know what kind, and I have outgrown paper dolls, but Jane Whitmore is more than just a paper doll.

Aunt Eveline sighed heavily and carried the Haviland cup to Aunt Kate, still fast asleep over her rosary. "Teatime, Katie, dear," she said cheerfully.

Aunt Eveline stood waiting for Aunt Kate to bob awake, but Aunt Kate's slightly hairy chin continued to rest on her lavender shoulder.

"Katie, dear, your coffee!" Aunt Kate didn't budge, and the Haviland cup began to rattle in the saucer.

"Katie, dear?" Aunt Eveline asked anxiously.

"*Aunt Kate! Wake up!*" I hollered.

Aunt Kate's eyelids fluttered open, and her fingers moved on along her rosary beads.

"Oh, what a scare!" Aunt Eveline said, one hand on her heart, the other still shaking as she gave the coffee to Aunt Kate. "I knew something was amiss the very minute I saw your fingers only as far as the second decade of your beads!" Aunt Kate always finishes the Glorious Mysteries before napping, the Sorrowful Mysteries before bedtime, and the Joyful Mysteries before rising. "What a good thing that when the Lord called you, you just told Him He'd have to wait a bit."

Aunt Kate chuckled. "For a vacancy in our second family home!" she said.

"Yes, indeed!" Aunt Eveline said happily. "Our second family home! But we have to move in one at a time! Everyone has to wait his turn. After all, Kate, Ben's only been gone six months, and even in our climate, that's just not long enough!"

It might as well have been a conversation in Chinese for all someone outside this house would understand. But

I knew they were talking about our tomb in Saint Louis #2 Cemetery.

"You mean Uncle Ben hasn't departed yet," I said. "De-parted. Get it?"

"Addie!" Aunt Eveline cried. "That is not an amusing pun."

"Well, it's the same thing you were just saying. There's only room for one body in the tomb, and if Uncle Ben hasn't turned to dust yet and sifted through the grating to the ground, there's no room for Aunt Kate."

"That will be quite enough, young lady!" Aunt Eveline swished her lavender skirt away from me.

I didn't really want to make her mad, so I tried again. "You're absolutely right about the second home part, Aunt Eveline. Those tombs in Saint Louis #2 look just like little houses. Sister Elizabeth Anne told us they had to build them above ground in the old days because New Orleans was so marshy we'd have floated away underneath. Can't you just see all those people we've buried floating away, right on out to the Gulf of Mexico where my mother —"

"Adelaide! Not another word!" Aunt Eveline's voice shook and squeaked.

Aunt Kate's white, pincushion head bobbed in a jolly way as she sipped her coffee and said, "What a *crowd* of people will come out of our tomb on the Last Day!"

"If only darling Pasie were with us!" Aunt Eveline said. She didn't mean with us on the mohair sofa, she meant with us in the crowd at Saint Louis #2.

"Just the same, you're always putting flowers on the tomb for my mother," I said. "It would make a lot more sense to throw them into the Gulf."

"Just like Harold's father!" piped up Sandra Lee,

7

coming through the door, yellow curls bouncing. I slipped Jane Whitmore out of sight into a magazine and casually put the scissors on the table. "Harold's father is going to sprinkle his ashes in the Mississippi River because he's a river pilot."

"Pagan!" Aunt Eveline glared at me as though I'd suggested it.

"I am sick to death of hearing about Harold," I snarled. Harold is in love with Sandra Lee and vice versa.

"I am speaking of Harold's *father*. I wonder what ever became of Tom's father?" Sandra Lee knows perfectly well that he just up and left home when Tom was a baby.

"It's not my business, I'm sure," I said. I am not in love with Tom or vice versa. "And I just meant sprinkling *flowers,* Aunt Eveline, into the Gulf, where my —"

"Adelaide, I do not wish to pursue the subject! An absolutely heathen thought! And please wear your hair so that it does not impair your vision." I glared at Sandra Lee and anchored my straight black hair at the sides with the bobby pins that had slipped. I can't help it if my bangs, which are in the process of growing out, do not look their best at the moment.

Sandra Lee smiled her dimples at me and tossed her golden curls. I tried to turn the other cheek, but I had run out of cheeks. "Harold must need glasses!" I had to whisper so Aunt Eveline wouldn't hear. "I've never seen a meaner-looking girl than you!"

Sandra Lee's lips curled at the corners and she looked at me with my mother's portrait eyes. "Heathen!" she mouthed so that only I could see.

Aunt Eveline helped Aunt Kate upstairs, and Sandra Lee skipped to the radio, singing off-key:

Who's that little chatterbox?
The one with pretty auburn locks?
Who can it be?
It's Little Orphan An-nie!

"Why is it," I asked, "that although you have a perfectly good radio right next door at your own house, you never miss listening to Little Orphan Annie here at my house?"

Cute little she,
It's Little Orphan An-nie!

Sandra Lee croaked the theme song, not even looking in my direction, and plopped down in what she considers her chair.

"My, my!" she said. "A paper doll! What would Tom say?" Jane Whitmore had fallen out of the magazine and was lying with her portrait dress on the floor. Sandra Lee snatched them up before I could.

"I don't care what Tom would say! Give it back! It's not a play doll! It's practice! I'm going to be——"

"I know. An artist. Just like your mother, Aunt Pasie." Sandra Lee was putting the portrait dress on Jane Whitmore. "Is this supposed to be Aunt Pasie? You've got her curves right, anyhow. Quite a girl. So I hear."

"What are you talking about? What did you hear?"

"Oh, nothing."

"Did Aunt Toosie tell you something about my mother?"

"My mother wouldn't say anything about her own sister! Hush! It's starting." Sandra Lee threw Jane Whitmore at me and unpinned her Little Orphan Annie Secret Society decoding badge.

Sandra Lee is a member of the Secret Society, and she got her badge by mailing two Ovaltine tops and ten cents to Little Orphan Annie. She got a book, too, with secret codes and Seven Golden Rules, which she obeys like the Ten Commandments, especially the Sixth, about drinking Ovaltine three times a day. Even if it weren't for the Sixth, Aunt Toosie would make Sandra Lee drink Ovaltine because she says Sandra Lee needs building up. It seems to me that if anyone needs "building up," it is a person built like a pencil, namely me, but Aunt Eveline says, "Golden Rules notwithstanding, Ovaltine is far too stimulating for young people."

At the end of the program, I watched Sandra Lee write down the numbers Little Orphan Annie broadcast. She spun the wheel on her badge and wrote letters next to the numbers. She saw me watching and hugged her paper to her chest. "I'm so sorry, Adelaide," she said, "but Outsiders aren't allowed to know the Secret Message."

I tried not to care, but I did. "Sandra Lee," I said humbly, "could I please have two of your extra Ovaltine tops to send off?"

"You're supposed to save your own," she said piously. "I have to be fair to Little Orphan Annie."

A wave of pure hate washed over me. "Why don't you just go home, then, to your old Ovaltine and your cute little organdy cottage and get out of my house!"

"I was leaving anyway," she snapped back. "And Three Twenty's not your house, it's Aunt Eveline's and Aunt Kate's, and they're as much my aunts as yours!"

"You can have this whole place for all I care!" I shouted. "It's practically haunted. You can take every last thing in it! All except the portrait."

"I don't even want the portrait!" Sandra Lee shouted back. "I wouldn't want a mother like that!"

"How's a body to cook with all that carrying on?" Nini cried, coming out of the kitchen. Nini, who has been our cook for twenty years, is the only sane person at Three Twenty Audubon Street.

"Oh, Nini," I wailed. Sandra Lee had made a quick exit, and I was fighting a losing battle with tears. "What was wrong with my mother?"

"Not one thing, honey," Nini said. "Not one thing wrong with your mother!"

"But didn't everyone love her?"

"Yes, indeed, they loved her! All your aunts, they *loved* her! Toosie, Kate, Eveline, especially your Aunt Eveline. Yes, indeed." Nini's dark face was serious, as if she were way back in time remembering how they all loved my mother. "And now, my girl, I fixed lost bread with plenty sugar for your supper. You just eat and pop up to bed. Your mother was a good girl. Yes, indeed. And what you needs is a good night's rest."

"If she was so good, what was Sandra Lee talking about?" I asked.

"How I know what that child got in her mind?" Nini said crossly. "You just get your rest. Eight whole hours your Aunt Eveline says. Your Aunt Eveline knows what's good for you."

If anyone in this house knows what's good for a girl practically thirteen, they're keeping it from me. My secret life as Jane Whitmore is absolutely the only thing that saves me from going mad. Every night after I go to bed, I block out my pencil figure, the straight black bangs, the Family Nose . . . I am Jane Whitmore. I smooth my golden curls and run my hand over my little turned-up nose, down my well-developed bust to my tiny waist. My favorite scene is Jane Whitmore in the Hurricane, in which, against incredible odds, Edmond Hilary de St. Denis rescues me from the giant waves. As he swims for shore, holding me half dead in his arms, I whisper in his ear, "Edmond, I cannot leave you! Your love is the bridge over which I trod back to life and to you!" His tears of joy are saltier than the waves.

Another good scene is Jane Whitmore Defies Death, in which I miraculously recover from a near-fatal disease, but not before I have soaked my pillow with real tears. I love the line, "Jane, my darling, you have returned to earth like Spring following Winter!"

After I finished seconds on the lost bread, I went upstairs and did my homework. After that, I went straight to bed to do Jane Whitmore Returns. I got so deep into it, I didn't hear Aunt Eveline come in. In this new scene, Edmond does not know I have come home after my two years of studying art in Florence, and he wanders into my one-man show by chance.

"Masterly," he murmurs, admiring my landscapes. Then, he sees my self-portrait and recognizes me! "Jane!" His manly voice breaks as he gazes at my likeness and realizes how much he wants to see me.

"Edmond!" I say, coming up behind him and placing one small hand on his arm. "I hardly knew you! You've grown a mustache!"

"What?" cried Aunt Eveline, making me jump a mile. "I may have a few hairs on my lip, but certainly not a mustache! Why is your hand dangling in the air?"

"My hand? Oh. I was half asleep. Talking in my sleep!"

"You've been crying!" Her voice softened. "Is it your mother, dear?"

"Yes." I produced more tears.

"Poor angel!" Aunt Eveline prepared to sit on the edge of my bed. "How could you help mourning your loss — that lovely girl, so young and beautiful! Her career and life in front of her! What a tragedy! If only she were in —"

"I'm all right now, Aunt Eveline," I said hurriedly. "I'm just fine now. I'm sure I'll sleep."

"We'll visit the Delgado, tomorrow, dear. Would you like that?"

"Oh, yes, Aunt Eveline!" Aunt Eveline knows I like going to the museum with her. She tells me about the lives of the artists and their paintings, because she used to be the art and debate teacher at Allen School until she retired to look after me. She still paints dog portraits, but they are pretty awful, even though they look like the dogs and make the owners happy.

"Well, good night, then, dear."

"Good night, Aunt Eveline."

Jane Whitmore doesn't work after interruptions, so when Aunt Eveline left, I tried to sleep, hoping I would not dream of the tidal wave that swept me, my mother and father, and our whole house into the Gulf of Mexico.

CHAPTER II

～～～～～～～～

"HELP! Mable, hel-up, 'm ch-chokin'! *May*-ble! Tom, get that critter outta here!"

"I'm coming, Malvern!" Tom's mother answered as Tom crashed through the hedge between our houses, tripped up my steps, and landed on the porch. He was clutching a mangy dog, even skinnier than he is.

"What in the world was your Uncle Malvern yelling about? That dog didn't bite him, did it?"

"Pumpkin wouldn't bite anybody! Uncle Malvern is allergic to dog hair. Stopped breathing when he saw Pumpkin — he says."

"He can still yell pretty good. That is the skinniest dog I ever saw."

"You'd be skinny, too, if the SPCA man had taken

your mother away and gone after you with a net. Poor little Pumpkin."

"Pumpkin? Why don't you call her Ribs?"

Tom ignored the insult. "She's almost the right color for a pumpkin, and Halloween's coming," he said. "Pumpkin's so smart, she hid until the SPCA left. I crawled under the house and rescued her, huh, Pumpkin, old girl? I rescued you!"

"What are you going to do with her?"

"Addie, what would you do if somebody gave you a choice between what you want most in the whole world, but you had to leave home forever to have it, or, you could never have that one thing, but you could stay at home and have almost anything else?"

"Well, if all you want is that dog you're holding, I wouldn't bother to leave home, even though you have to put up with your uncle and his beer."

"I don't *want* to leave. But I will if I have to. Unless . . . unless . . ." Tom and Pumpkin were looking at me.

"Tom, I can't keep that dog for you! Aunt Eveline would have a fit. *And* Aunt Kate! Why, Aunt Kate'd die right on the spot. Honest. I can *not!*"

I noticed Tom's hair and freckles matched Pumpkin's coat. There is definitely no resemblance between Tom and Edmond Hilary de St. Denis.

"Addie, just for a while! I'm right next door, and I'll be the one really taking care of her — until I talk my mother into keeping her. I'll do anything you want. What do you want most in the world?"

"You can't give me what I want most in the world."

"Aw, come on, Addie! Aunt Eveline will let you keep good old Pumpkin if you beg her. Just for a while."

"No."

"Well, Addie, so long, then! I'm leaving," said Tom, not going. "Good-bye."

I knew he was still working on me, but I didn't want a mangy dog. Pumpkin didn't look anything like my mother's cute little Fifi.

"I'll be seeing you, Addie."

"That's crazy. Where will you go?"

"North Carolina."

"What'll you do there?"

"Live there. With my dog."

"Tom, your mother needs you to help with your uncle. Besides, Pumpkin isn't all that great a dog."

Tom's freckles changed color and his mouth turned thin white.

"Now, Tom, I didn't mean Pumpkin wasn't a good dog!" Tom's eyes were making holes right through me. "It's just that I know what Aunt Eveline would say —"

"Good-bye, Addie."

"Tom, now listen, Tom!"

Pumpkin let out a bark that sounded like good-bye.

"It's been great knowing you," Tom said.

"Wait, Tom!"

"Ah-de-la-eed!" Aunt Eveline was calling me. "Addie, dear!"

"Tom! Listen!" I was looking at the back of Tom with the back of Pumpkin tucked under his arm.

"Adelaide, when I call, please reply immediately. Addie, I want you to —"

"Aunt Eveline, what would you say if someone gave you a choice: you could keep me, but you had to keep something else you didn't want besides; or, you'd lose me and you could have anything else in the whole world you want."

"I only want you, dear."

16

"You don't want anything else? I thought you wanted my mother to be buried in Saint Louis #2."

"I must be content with things as they are, dear."

"Then, you'd choose me and the other thing you didn't want besides?"

"I'd choose you above all else, dear, although I still nourish the hope that you will someday decide on a length for your bangs. Now, what I want you to do, Addie, is —"

"My bangs are almost grown out, Aunt Eveline, and I'm glad you want me above all things, because I do need this other thing to be happy and I'm pleased you've chosen it."

"I was not aware of choosing this other thing. What is it?"

"I can have it, can't I?"

"I'm sure you *can*, but perhaps you *may* not. What is it?"

"Oh, Aunt Eveline! It's a matter of life or death! Can I — *may* I have a dog? A *very* small one. She's smart and I promise I'll take care of her."

"A dog! Of course not! Absolutely not! Aunt Kate would —"

"I won't let Pumpkin bother Aunt Kate. I promise!"

"Oh, Addie! How could you do that?"

"I'll keep her in my room."

"Inside?"

"I'll keep her outside. In the shed! Oh, *please,* Aunt Eveline!"

"Oh, Addie!"

"My mother had a dog."

"Fifi was sweet and very clean."

"Pumpkin is sweet, too, Aunt Eveline."

"Where is this dog?"

"I'll get it! Oh, you'll see! You'll *love* Pumpkin! *Tom!* *Hey, Tom! Wait! You don't have to go to North Carolina! Taw-m!*"

"*Please*, Adelaide! Don't howl like a banshee!"

Pumpkin wasn't exactly Fifi the Second, but maybe if I bathed her and fattened her up and Tom taught her a few tricks . . .

"Hey, Tom!" I ran down the street after Tom.

CHAPTER III

~~~~~~~~~~~~~~~~~~~~~~~~~~~~~

YOU CAN FIND your way around Three Twenty Audubon Street with your nose. Downstairs is cabbage, except for the mohair sofa, which is mothball, and the kitchen, which besides cabbage is Nini's roux, the burnt flour and fat smell that begins her creole cooking. Upstairs is pure cloves.

When I woke up the next morning, I fanned my room to make it clove-free. Aunt Kate's room is next to mine and she has an ancient potpourri, a jar of faded rose leaves and spices, all completely drowned out by the cloves. The cloves smell was seeping under the door into my room. I could tell Pumpkin was allergic to cloves by the way she was running around sniffing for fresh air. I stuffed the crack with newspaper, but after breakfast, when Aunt Eveline inspected my room to see if I'd made my bed, she pulled the newspaper out with a long lecture on promises made and not kept.

"The dog must remain outside, Adelaide. It smells very doggy in this room."

"You smell cloves, not Pumpkin. The cloves stink."

"Addie, do not use that word!"

"But I can't even smell my Fatal Moment," I said, unstopping my perfume and dabbing little drops of it behind my ears, at my elbows, and on my wrists. "It's all covered over by cloves, and Pumpkin almost suffocated last night!"

"Adelaide, I smell no cloves whatsoever, and I am quite aware of your perfume when you douse yourself in that liberal fashion, totally unsuitable for a school day. Kindly put that dog in the shed. I will look in on her while you're at school," she added in a kinder tone.

I brought Pumpkin to the shed, curled her up on my pillow, and closed the gate Tom had made from an old crate. On my way back upstairs I saw Aunt Eveline in the kitchen, putting scraps in a bowl for Pumpkin.

Aunt Eveline is not so bad when she tries. Aunt Kate, on the other hand, is just too old to change. She is a whole generation older than my mother and Sandra Lee's. Part of Aunt Kate seems already to have gone on to her reward, as Aunt Eveline puts it, and the other part is preparing. Never mind, Aunt Eveline says, she is laying up her treasure in Heaven, where her place is being made ready by those who have gone on before. There's a lot of activity up there, I thought, stepping into my school dress and looking at the photograph of my grandmother, lost among children of all sizes, her own and older ones belonging to my grandfather's first wife. One of the older girls in the picture is holding the baby of the family. The older girl is Aunt Eveline.

"Addie, you'll be late for school!" Aunt Eveline called up the steps. "Finish dressing and don't dawdle!"

The baby in the picture is my mother. I tied my shoes and wondered why I've never learned to say "was" instead of "is" for my mother. It has been such a long time since my mother, father, and I lived in Honduras. My father was manager of a banana plantation there and my mother painted landscapes, until one day, a hurricane came along, and a tidal wave swept most of Belize and our house into the Gulf. My father saved me, but, in Aunt Eveline's version of what happened, my mother was torn from his arms and hurled into the arms of the angels. I can't remember any of it — a strange, funny thing when I stop to think how dramatic it must have been.

"Ad-die! I see Sandra Lee on the steps already! What are you doing up there?"

"I'm dressing, Aunt Eveline!"

Aunt Eveline says my father died soon after of a broken heart, but the Honduran medical report called it malaria. I try to remember the bearded man whose picture sits on my dresser, but he is a stranger. He looks much older than my mother; I think he was closer to Aunt Eveline's age. None of it makes any difference, because I lost both of my parents and came to live here at Three Twenty instead of in a normal house with a mother and father.

"*Ah-de-la-eed! Are* you ready?"

"I'm coming, Aunt Eveline!"

Having Sandra Lee complete with parents and a normal house right next door makes it all ten times worse. Aunt Toosie and Uncle Henry's cozy cottage is full of chintz, organdy, and fake Early American furniture. They never listen to opera on the radio. They play dance music on the phonograph, and once I even saw them roll back the rug and dance cheek to cheek.

"At last!" Aunt Eveline said at the foot of the steps. "I sincerely hope you don't make Sandra Lee, who was ready on time, miss the bell. Your hair! But never mind, I see her waiting very patiently in front of her house."

I don't like to criticize Aunt Eveline or Aunt Kate, but they could take a lesson from Aunt Toosie and her cute cottage. Three Twenty, although free of cobwebs, is definitely spooky, with carved wood curling around everything you sit on and heavy brocade draperies choking the light out of the windows.

"Now, Addie, be sure and buy milk for lunch. No Coke."

"Don't forget to feed Pumpkin, Aunt Eveline."

I stopped suddenly on my way out the door. A plan had just occurred to me. "Aunt Eveline, we need a giant yard sale. I would start in the attic, if I were you, and work to the ground, and when we have everything out on the lawn, I'll holler, 'Come and get it!' Then we'll seal off the attic permanently, fumigate the rest of the house, and then, well, to tell you the truth, the easiest thing will be to sell Three Twenty and move miles away from Sandra Lee."

Aunt Eveline got all upset and failed to see the benefits of my plan. Aunt Kate said if my mother were alive, I'd be living in a jungle, and how would I like that, and Aunt Eveline calmed down and said that the colors are beautiful in Honduras, and I would have loved to paint there. I left for school before anything else could worry her, and she stood on the porch, smiling and waving, dressed all in lavender.

Aunt Toosie was out on her porch, too, in a dress of pink and white checks. Sandra Lee shook her head so that her yellow curls bounced. She looked at me through her long lashes and twitched her little nose in a shy smile, all for Aunt Eveline's benefit. I didn't get another smile out of her the whole school day.

That afternoon I was sitting at my dressing table, doing my nose-shortening exercise. Aunt Eveline says I have my father's Family Nose and it is very aristocratic, but I'd like it better if it were less aristocratic and more like the one in my mother's portrait. So I'm shortening it. I had a piece of adhesive tape across the bridge to keep my nose from humping, and another stuck on the sides and looped under like a sling to lift it. I had been sitting there for five minutes and my nose was just starting to shorten, when I heard Aunt Eveline clumping up the steps and heading straight for my closed door. I ripped off the adhesive tape and pretended to be combing my hair.

No knock.

"Addie, dear, I baked cookies for you and Sandra Lee to take to Sister Elizabeth Anne when you go for catechism. 'Who made me?' "

" 'God made me,' " I snapped back like a parrot.

" 'Why did God make you?' " Aunt Eveline not only knows the answers, she knows all of the questions in the Baltimore Catechism.

" 'God made me to know Him, to love Him, and to serve Him in this world, and to be happy with Him in the next.' " Not a preposition out of place.

"Good. Your nose is red. What happened to it?"

"Nothing. It's not red." If I said I had a cold, she'd give me milk of magnesia and put me to bed.

"It is *too* red." Sandra Lee's face popped around the

door. "And swollen! What are those two pieces of adhesive tape for?"

She had come in my house and up the stairs silently, and I knew from the expression on her face that she already knew what the adhesive tape was for, and that, therefore, she must have been looking through the keyhole. You just don't get any sneakier than that!

By that time, my whole face was red, but Aunt Eveline was off on her favorite subjects, cleanliness and manners.

"Now, Addie, wash your hands after playing with that dog." Aunt Eveline couldn't get in the habit of calling Pumpkin by her name. "And please remember to say 'Yes' and 'No, Sister Elizabeth Anne,' and not 'uh-huh' and 'un-un.' And, Addie, comb your hair before you leave. It looks like a bird's nest."

Before Aunt Eveline could come up with suggestions of what to do so that my hair would look less like "monk in the bush," I hurried to the bathroom, splashed water on my hands, slapped my hair with a brush, and, tearing back through my room, grabbed my catechism, charged down the steps, and banged the screen door as hard as possible so that, with a little luck, it would hit Sandra Lee as she followed close behind me, smirking and twitching her little nose.

The nuns that teach our school live at the end of our block, and Sister Elizabeth Anne is always waiting for us on the front porch in a caned rocker, her rosary in her hands, her slightly crossed eyes looking more or less in our direction. Aunt Kate says one eye is looking at Heaven, but I have never been able to decide which one. There are two empty rockers next to Sister Elizabeth Anne, and we sit down in a row facing front, rocking and staring through the screen.

The lessons are a special favor to Aunt Kate from Sister Elizabeth Anne, who went to school with Aunt Kate. Sandra Lee and I have already been confirmed after years of catechism, but this, in Aunt Kate's opinion, is not enough insurance against the ever-present threat of heathenism.

" 'Why did God make you?' "

" 'God made me [rock] to know Him [rock] and to love Him [rock] and to serve him in this world [rock, rock] and to be happy with Him in the next [rock, rock, rock].' " I could say it backwards.

" 'Who is God?' "

"Uh [rock, rock] uh, 'God is' [rock] 'God is the creator of' uh, [rock, rock] of uh, [nose twitching, lashes batting] uh . . ."

" 'God is the creator of Heaven and' ?"

" 'God is the creator of Heaven and' uh . . . [rock, rock] and uh . . ."

" 'And earth and' ?"

"Uh, 'and earth and' uh . . ."

" '*God is the creator of Heaven and earth and all things*!'" I shouted.

"You must let Sandra Lee have a turn," Sister Elizabeth Anne said.

After half an hour of rocking, uh-ing, and nose twitching, Sister Elizabeth Anne stood up, satisfied we knew the lesson. I tried to pretend I wasn't in a hurry to leave and edged forward in my rocker slowly. Sandra Lee pretended she was having such a good time she hated to leave. Gazing up through her lashes and smiling shyly, she leaned back in the rocker and rocked forward on my toe.

I leaped in the air, banging into Sister Elizabeth Anne.

Something fell to the floor with a tinkling sound. The silver heart that is supposed to hang from Sister Elizabeth Anne's starched white scapula was lying at my feet.

"An omen!" she cried, smiling at me. "Someday, perhaps, you will become a nun!"

Sandra Lee piously crossed herself and said sweetly, "Amen!"

I stared in horror at Sister Elizabeth Anne, draped in black, every hair on her head trapped inside a kind of religious helmet. Me, a nun? What about Edmond? My art? My mouth hung open while I silently prayed, Please, God, don't make any mistakes about me. Let my secret life come true and let me develop and — and make Sandra Lee a nun.

I forgot to say good-bye and thank you, and ran home.

"Holly's coming!" Nini said before I could get the screen door open. "And Tom says he took Pumpkin to the park. And ain't it wonderful that Holly's coming?" Usually, you can sit in Nini's kitchen, thinking your own thoughts while she moves around singing "Pack Up Your Troubles" or some other World War song, but today, she couldn't stop talking about her granddaughter from Chicago. She sipped her café au lait and nibbled at bread spread with cane syrup, her steady diet.

"Wait till you see Holly! That's some girl! Smart, just like you!"

"Nini," I asked, bored with Holly, who wasn't coming for another week, "when my mother was growing up, was she like me?"

"No," she answered shortly.

"Sandra Lee said she was quite a girl."

Nini looked at me sharply. "What she mean by that?"

"I'm asking *you* what she means."

Nini's dark eyes, matted in pure white and framed in

her black face, took in all of me. "You just keep to your business," she said. "Ain't no use digging at the past."

"Well, I'd just like to be like her, that's all, my own mother, and how can I be when you won't tell me what she was like and I never knew her?"

"How you ever gonna know her when she's dead? You just aim to be like your Aunt Eveline, that's what," Nini said crossly.

"Why?"

"A happy woman, that's why."

"I don't think I want to be like Aunt Eveline," I said carefully. "I am sure I will never wear lavender."

"Lavender means grieving. Nothing wrong with grieving when the time comes."

"Yes, but Aunt Eveline and Aunt Kate are always grieving — they're always mourning for somebody! They start off in black, which *has* to be worn exactly one year for fathers, mothers, husbands, or wives, six months for sisters and brothers, and three for cousins, then they 'go into lavender,' and they never do get past lavender to real colors before black sets in again!"

Nini laughed at me. "Your Aunt Eveline was young once — just like you — and your mama — and she had a laugh like this." Nini tapped a crystal glass with a spoon. "Until — but if you want to stand there gabbin', hand me that polish and here's your cloth, and we'll get this silver shining before Holly comes."

The very thought of her granddaughter put Nini back in a good humor, but I was tired of hearing about Holly since I had never even seen her. I gobbled my peanut butter, mayonnaise, and banana sandwich, rubbed one spoon, and went upstairs to draw.

I started off drawing clothes for Jane Whitmore. I remembered a snapshot Aunt Kate has of my mother that she keeps in her tin box of souvenirs. In the snapshot, my mother is waving from the deck of the ship that took her across the ocean. She is wearing a fur coat, and a hat so low on her forehead that her face is in shadow. I drew a cloche hat for Jane Whitmore.

It bothers me that I have to look at pictures to know what my mother looked like and ask other people to tell me about her. I wish I could remember her for myself, but I can't remember anything before my sixth birthday — nothing about my mother, my father, or the hurricane. It doesn't bother me as much about my father. I guess I miss him. I know I would if I could remember him, but it's as though my memory was born the day I sat down at the heavy oak table at Three Twenty Audubon Street and saw a pile of neatly wrapped birthday presents surrounded by a garland of butterfly lilies and four-o'clocks. I remember exactly that one of my presents was a lace-trimmed handkerchief with *A* embroidered in the corner and a paper sticker that said PURE IRISH LINEN. Everything that happened before that is lost, as though the tidal wave had swept it away with our house. A terrible dream about the wave comes again and again, so real I can't tell if it's a nightmare or a memory.

Suddenly, I realized I had stopped drawing clothes for Jane Whitmore and was drawing male profiles, and, yes! there he was, Edmond Hilary de St. Denis, cleft chin, blue, steady eyes (or eye, I should say, since it was his profile), sensitive mouth, and short straight nose. He was absolutely beautiful, the best thing I had ever done. I pulled out a *Photoplay* magazine from the stack I have, ripped the inside out, and pasted the tops and bottoms of the cover to form an envelope. I hid Edmond inside and slid the cover in between two other *Photoplays*.

I heard Aunt Eveline coming out of her room, so I

quickly slid Jane Whitmore and her new clothes into the envelope with Edmond and picked up a book.

When Aunt Eveline came in I asked, "Aunt Eveline, did my mother learn a lot in Florence?"

"Oh, yes! She loved Florence, and her professor considered her most talented. Most talented!"

"I wish I had one of her paintings."

"Unfortunately, dear, she did her mature work in Honduras and her watercolors were all lost in the hurricane when your house was washed away. Naturally, your father only had time to try to save you and your mother. We have only her early watercolors! Exercises, really."

I had seen the exercises in a box in the attic.

"All of the good ones were lost?" I asked. "Every single one?"

"I'm so sorry, dear! But — well — as a matter of fact, I do have one! Yes, one. In my armoire. I'll get it."

Just like that! I followed Aunt Eveline into her room. It was a place I seldom entered. There was not a trace of cloves. Only fresh air and the expensive scent of Roget and Gaillet soap, Aunt Eveline's one concession to luxury.

Aunt Eveline opened the heavy armoire door, and I saw a pile of watercolor papers neatly stacked on a shelf. Aunt Eveline picked up the top one and then, noticing for the first time that I was standing right behind her, she quickly closed the door.

"Here, dear. Your mother did this."

I held a landscape of the lagoon in Audubon Park. The colors were pastel and overlapped in some places, blending together into deeper shades that gave me the feeling I could walk right into the painting. It was a fresh and happy watercolor, a moment caught forever by an artist who knew how to paint.

"Oh," was all I said.

"You don't like it?" Aunt Eveline asked anxiously.

"I love it," I said unhappily. "It's just that — I'll never be that good."

"Of course you will, my dear! You have her talent and you will get training — the very best. Don't forget, this is your mother's mature work, at the peak of her power. She didn't do anything as finished as this at your age."

"Could I have it?"

Aunt Eveline hesitated only a minute before saying, "Of course, my dear. We'll have it framed."

CHAPTER IV

～～～～～～～～～

THE DAY AFTER Aunt Eveline gave me my mother's watercolor, we had dancing school.

"No, no, *no!*" Miss Rush clapped her hands to stop Miss Morrison at the piano. "Sandra Lee! Listen! And *one* and two and one and two — and *one* . . . Now, begin! And *one* . . . *Sandra Lee, no!*" Miss Rush looks at arms and hands, feet and legs. No amount of lash-batting and nose-twitching diverted her attention from Sandra Lee's jerky hands and stubby feet moving in opposition to the rhythm of the music.

I loved the dumb look on Sandra Lee's face.

Miss Rush turned away from Sandra Lee. "All right, Miss Morrison, begin again. And *one* and two and — good, Addie!"

Sandra Lee continued to fight the music and the tears forming in her eyes. It would be different Friday night when we have ballroom dancing with boys. The boys love Sandra Lee. They don't notice her hands and feet; they fall for all her fakiness. Harold always asks her a week in advance for the contest. She doesn't know what it's like to have to duck in the back before the contest starts, or talk with another girl, laughing and pretending you don't want a partner.

Prominent among the wallflowers is Denise, who, when bent like the letter *C*, remains four inches taller than the tallest boy; Elizabeth, who wears glasses as thick as Coke bottles; and me, shaped like a pencil. Our personalities, no matter how jolly we make them, do not make up for the physical realities — nor for Aunt Eveline.

"Aunt Eveline, no one will wear a dress like this!" I was standing on a box while Aunt Eveline pinned the hem up.

"That's just it! This dress is an original Lily Dior. Your mother wore only lovely things, and, in its day, this dress was all the rage. You don't want to look like everyone else at dancing school, do you?"

"Yes."

"Now, Adelaide, what makes you interesting is being different from others. Being yourself."

"Sandra Lee isn't different. She's more like everyone else than anyone I know and she's popular."

"I'm sure you're popular, too, dear."

"I'm not! Tom is the only one who dances with me, and he just does it because the teachers make him. Half the time I don't get a partner for the contest, and I have to pretend I love talking to Denise and Elizabeth. We laugh and act like we're having so much fun, and the teachers come over and ask how our parents are. Aunt Eveline, what can I say to make the boys like me?"

"Just be yourself, dear. Boys will like you. After all, you don't want every Tom, Dick, and Harry crazy about you."

"Yes, I do!"

"Addie, that's common. Now, hold still while I pin this hem."

"Aunt Eveline, did my mother have a lot of boyfriends?"

"Certainly not!" Aunt Eveline exclaimed, shocked. "She had many male acquaintances, but her only 'boyfriend,' as you so quaintly put it, was your dear father. There now," she added, standing back.

I looked at myself in the mirror. The dusty-rose gown gave my skin a sallow color. The V-neck, decorated by a huge rhinestone brooch, showed that my chest was only a chest, and the accordion pleats, hanging from my shoulders to the floor without a ripple, proved there were no curves anywhere. I might just as well have been a boy. Please, Lord, let me develop, just a little. I promise I will never . . .

"Perfect! Simply elegant!" exclaimed Aunt Eveline. Was she blind? Was I missing something? I looked again, and there, reflected behind me, was Sandra Lee, with an expression on her face that told me everything I feared was true.

"Aunt Eveline," I said, "thank you so much! It's just perfect! It's not every little girl who can wear a Lily Dior to dancing school!"

Sandra Lee's expression faltered. That girl was dumb! You could make her think anything.

"It looks Grecian, don't you think?" I said gaily to

Aunt Eveline, ignoring Sandra Lee. I swung around, hoping to create a swirling effect, but the stubborn pleats only buckled slightly and then fell into permanent straightness.

"Not Grecian. Venetian," said Aunt Kate from the hall.

"Venice?" asked Aunt Eveline, puzzled.

"Blind. Venetian blind," said Aunt Kate, toddling on down the hall to the Glorious Mysteries.

It was too great an effort to pretend anymore. I made up my mind that I would at least do away with the shield that passed for a brooch. As I pulled the Lily Dior over my head, I caught a whiff of the perfume that clings to all of my mother's things. My mother had worn this dress, but on her it must have revealed, in a modest way, of course, her tiny waist and curves.

"God's nightgown!" said Tom on Friday night. One of the chaperones had pried him loose from the wall and shoved him in my direction in the middle of the third dance. He pulled me to the dance floor, and holding me as though I were contagious, started shouting to overcome the noise of the piano and the distance separating us. "Your dress looks like a nightgown! It is a dress, isn't it?" he yelled, swooping me across the floor in a giant box step.

"It's a Lily Dior," I whispered.

"A what?"

"A Lily Dior." If I spoke low enough maybe he'd notice that the whole dancing school could hear him.

"Somebody doesn't know the difference between night and day! Did you finish *Lad?*"

"I'm not deaf, Tom," I said, giving up, and shouting

back. "I'll bring it back tomorrow. Do you mind if I borrow the next one?"

"You can read them all. Doesn't Pumpkin remind you of Lad? I'm training Pumpkin to be just like him. She'll . . ."

But the piano stopped, releasing Tom from dancing and conversation, and he retreated to the wall in mid-sentence. Holding my head like Jane Whitmore, I marched toward the back room, trying not to look abandoned.

"Stuck-up!" Harold hissed at me.

"So what?" I snapped back. Let him be in love with Sandra Lee, I didn't care. Not one of those boys even vaguely resembled Edmond. Tom least of all, with his freckles and straw hair and long, skinny arms and legs. He only danced with me because his mother was a friend of my family, and she told him he had to. I didn't care if any of those boys liked me or not. Especially Harold.

"Addie, what are you doing back here?" Miss Rush came in just as Edmond was about to discover me, dressed in my simple white dress.

"Uh, nothing."

"I saw you dancing with Tom. He's a nice boy, isn't he?"

"His mother or somebody probably made him."

"Told him to dance with you? Nonsense! He chose you."

I refused to answer such an obvious lie. I guess Miss Rush saw I was close to tears, because she turned sincere.

"Addie, dear, don't worry if no one asks you for the contest. You're going to be lovely when you grow up! How well I remember your beautiful mother! And — and, I'm going to speak to Eveline about your clothes —

35

now! Good heavens!" Words failed her as she contemplated the Lily Dior.

"It's a Lily Dior," I said timidly.

"It's terrible. But you! Those eyes and that figure!"

Family Nose, I thought. What figure?

"Eveline told me you like to draw. Are you going to be an artist?"

"Maybe." I hate conversations with grown people where they pretend to be interested in me. "Miss Rush, I'm going home now."

"Oh, no, dear! You can't leave before your Aunt Toosie comes for you!" she said in alarm. "I'll call you the minute she gets here."

I don't like pity, either, so I didn't say anything, but when Miss Rush gave up and went back to judge the contest, sure to be won by Sandra Lee and dumb Harold, I slipped out the back into the warm, moist air and mooncloudy night.

When I got home, crawled into bed, and tried to enter into my secret life, Aunt Eveline came in, supposedly to tuck me in, but actually to pry out of me why I'd left dancing school before Aunt Toosie came.

"What's wrong, dear?" she said a million times in tragic tones. "Is it your mother?"

"No," I snapped. "It is not my mother or anything else. Everything is fine and I am sleepy. Good night."

I rolled over, making further conversation impossible, and she finally left.

"Jane! Jane, my darling!" Edmond whispered lovingly to me, but I was too tired to answer, and fell asleep, straight into my giant-wave nightmare. It begins with Fear. Just the feeling. I don't know why I'm afraid and I try to figure out what is terrifying me. Then I hear it — a great roaring noise coming closer, and I know it is the sound of a tidal wave twenty feet, fifty feet high, rolling in out of the Gulf of Mexico. I try to run but my legs go in movie slow motion. It is too late to get away. I see the wave coming toward me, towering over my head, cresting and breaking with a mighty crash, swallowing me into its green underbelly. I look up through miles of transparent water, unable to move my arms or legs. I know my mother is near, but if I open my mouth to call, I'll swallow water. I hold my breath until real panic and the need to breathe wake me, gasping for air and sobbing with relief.

CHAPTER V

~~~~~~~~~~~~~~~~~~

"A DDIE! Addie! Is Pumpkin with you?"

"No," I said, desperately trying to remember exactly what I'd done when I left the shed before school. I was sure I'd closed the gate we keep across the door — wasn't I? "I'm positive I closed the gate," I said, not positive.

"No use what you did, child." Nini had come out on the porch. "Tom, your Uncle Malvern done let Pumpkin out first thing this morning. Came in this yard with a handkerchief tied round his face like a thief mask! 'Nina!' he say. Can't never get my name straight. 'Gotta borrow this here dog for a few years!' He laughed like he's making a big joke. 'Mr. Malvern,' I say, 'I wouldn't mess with Pumpkin if I was you.' 'But you ain't me,' he say, 'and you ain't allergic to dog hair.' So he goes in the shed and next thing I know, he's running out, yelling he been bit and he can't breathe, and Pumpkin is a-chasing him and I ain't seen Pumpkin since."

Tom didn't say a word. He turned and ran to his house. I ran after him. I caught up outside Uncle Malvern's door. Uncle Malvern was standing there saying, "Shore sorry, boy. Didn't mean for her to get away. Thought I'd take her to a place I know in the country for a day or so. Country air, ya know. A dog needs country air."

Tom's fist was clenched and I'm not sure what he would have done. We heard a bark. There was no mistake. It was Pumpkin. Tom took the back steps, using the handrail to swing himself down in two leaps, and I found him hugging Pumpkin, who was licking him and wagging the whole back half of herself. She knew she was Tom's dog even though she lived at my house. I watched and thought, Pumpkin has a nice face and her ribs don't show anymore, but, well, the truth is, she'll never be pretty. "Too bad she's so ugly!" I said, not thinking.

Tom turned on me. "The trouble with you is, you don't care about anything! Nothing that counts. It's not how she *looks* that counts! And you're the same with people. They're nice to you and you're not nice to them. You just don't *care!*"

I just stood there with my mouth open. I started to be mad, but the truth of what he'd said sunk in. I knew what he meant. I really didn't care. Not about Pumpkin or Aunt Eveline or anyone. Except — myself. I burst into tears.

"Aw, Addie, come on, now. Don't cry! I'm sorry. I didn't mean to make you *cry!*" Tom pushed a crumpled, only half-dirty handkerchief in my face. I cried all the more. First, because he had turned nice and I couldn't help it; then, because I realized I was having a good time.

"I'm sorry, Tom. I shouldn't have said that about Pumpkin. Maybe she will be beautiful someday. I'm so sorry, Tom!" A flood of tears.

"Addie, I *know* you are! Don't cry! Look, look, here's something for you." Tom was handing me a piece of bubble gum. He grinned when he saw I'd stopped crying long enough to see what he had. "Chew it," he said. "You can't chew and cry at the same time!" Tom has a nice smile. It reminded me just a very little bit of Edmond. I smiled back. He put his arm around me and pulled me to him. I sighed and put my head on his shoulder. He held me tight and put his mouth close to my ear and whispered, "Addie?"

"What?" I asked, breathless.

"It makes me feel good to know — to know Pumpkin came back to me."

Pumpkin wiggled herself between us and kissed me. Oh, Edmond, my darling! Forgive me for being unfaithful!

CHAPTER VI

A FEW DAYS LATER, it was Aunt Kate's birthday and
the whole family was coming to dinner. Aunt
Toosie and Uncle Henry had invited an out-of-town
friend called Edgar, and Aunt Eveline was fussing about
having a "guest," which was dumb because there were
already a dozen guests invited, relatives so far removed,
no one could remember where they fit into the family.

"Malvern is a guest, too, Eveline," Aunt Toosie said
peevishly. "If you only wanted family, why did you have
to ask him?"

Sandra Lee and I were weaving the garland of four-
o'clocks and butterfly lilies to go around Aunt Kate's
plate, and Sandra Lee stopped to give her opinion.
"Yes," she said, "why ask *Tom's* Uncle Malvern?"

I gave Sandra Lee a look that said children should be seen and not heard.

"I invited Tom's uncle and his mother as well," Aunt Eveline said. "After all, Malvern and Mable are *close* friends of this family, and they live next door. They're really not guests at all."

"Don't tell me Mable's coming!" Aunt Toosie cried.

"Mable declined."

"Of course she did! She hasn't set foot out of that house since Louis left home. She's Malvern's slave! Tom's at school all day and —"

"Yes, and he leaves his dog at our house," said Miss Butinsky.

"My house," I said.

"Please, girls!" Aunt Eveline said. "Now, Toosie, Malvern is working on his perpetual motion machine."

"You mean he's working on seeing how much alcohol the human body can take! And Mable waits on him hand and foot — cooking and scrubbing the house."

"She might try scrubbing Tom for a change," Sandra Lee butted in again.

"Just what is meant by that?" I asked. "At least Tom doesn't grease up his hair like some people I know."

"Harold does not 'grease up his hair.' He smooths it down with a very expensive, *non*greasy tonic!"

"It smells like old bubble gum!" I said. "It stinks like an old train station!"

"Adelaide!" cried Aunt Eveline, all excited. "I cannot abide that word! There will be no further discussion, and you're bruising the butterfly lilies you have clutched in your hand."

"How does this look, Aunt Eveline?" asked Sandra Lee sweetly, standing back from the garland we'd both made.

"Lovely, dear! Addie, please go into the garden and pick fresh lilies to replace those you've crushed."

I tried to catch Sandra Lee's eye on my way out so she'd see how I felt about her, but she had her eyes demurely cast down.

"I just haven't liked Malvern ever since he went to —" began Aunt Toosie again.

"Don't dawdle, Addie, dear," Aunt Eveline interrupted in the loud voice she uses to drown out interesting things I'm not supposed to hear. "Toosie, I'm certain Malvern will be the life of the party."

At one o'clock, we all sat down in the cabbage dining room. Aunt Kate's place looked special with the garland Sandra Lee and I had made, and a pile of presents to be opened before soup was ladled out of the tureen. Aunt Kate slowly unwrapped each present, saving for last the annual box of monogrammed handkerchiefs from Aunt Eveline.

"Exactly what I wanted, my dear!" she said, although she had a drawerful upstairs.

Cousin Jeannette, who, like a Christmas ornament taken down from the attic, appears on special days and disappears afterward, squeaked, "I have a little thought for you on my armoire shelf, Katie, dear!" There are thoughts on Cousin Jeannette's shelf for everyone's birthday, but not one has ever materialized.

I watched Uncle Malvern slurp his soup. I wondered if Tom missed his father as much as I missed my mother. I'd seen a picture of my mother with Tom's father. "Louis and me," she'd written on the back. Uncle Malvern was a poor substitute for a father, even one who had left home for no good reason.

Uncle Malvern was showing no signs of being the life of the party. In fact, the party was barely alive when, in the middle of the first course, orange-colored soup, Aunt Kate put her heavy spoon down and cried, "Give it to Esther!" There was no one named Esther at the table or anywhere else, as far as our startled guest, Edgar, could tell, but a thousand years ago when Aunt Kate boarded at the convent, there had been a girl called Esther who ate everything no one else wanted. The family knew Aunt Kate meant she didn't want any more soup.

Politely trying to cover up the general embarrassment, Edgar asked, "Is that lovely girl in the portrait you, Miss Eveline?"

Before Aunt Eveline could answer, Tom's uncle said, "Oh, no, that's Pasie. Lovely, isn't she?" He raised his wineglass. "To Pasie!"

Aunt Eveline was beaming. She raised her glass, but Uncle Malvern wasn't waiting for any of the others. He drained his glass as Aunt Eveline wound up for her model-of-perfection speech: "And a talented artist —"

Uncle Malvern, red-faced and chuckling, interrupted, "Yes, she may have been an artist, but she seldom drew the line! Ha, ha, ha!"

There was a terrible stillness, filled with Aunt Eveline's shocked anger. Uncle Malvern, still smiling stupidly, was the only one who didn't notice.

Uncle Henry jumped in quickly. "That one came straight out of *College Humor,* Malvern! Read it last week. By the way, Edgar, did you see where Drew Pearson, that Washington journalist, said Huey would have been President if he hadn't been assassinated?"

Everyone was happy to start arguing over whether or not the former governor of our state, Huey Long, had really had a chance for the presidency. *"A lunatic!"* Aunt Eveline said. The rest thought she meant Long, but I knew she hadn't paid a bit of attention to the conversation. She meant Uncle Malvern.

If all that wasn't embarrassing enough, just as Edgar was complimenting Aunt Kate on the Haviland china, Aunt Eveline turned to him and said, "Will you stay for tea? We always have coffee at Three Twenty around five." The poor man stared at her, then at his watch, while Aunt Eveline smiled and waited for an answer, and Sandra Lee choked on a laugh.

"It's the house number," I said, having trouble keeping my voice even. "We live at Three Twenty Audubon Street and tea means coffee." I stood up quickly and rushed from the room, so embarrassed I wanted to die.

I shoved open the swinging kitchen door before anyone could see my tears and ran into Nini carrying a serving dish full of peas. They rolled all over the floor. I tried to pick them up, and my fingers met a dirty saddle shoe. I looked up at a brown leg, a blue and green plaid dress, and a face that was Nini's minus about forty years. It was Holly. She didn't say anything; she handed me the broom and stood waiting with the dustpan. I smeared some tears and a pea across my cheek and started sweeping. Still not speaking, Holly squatted down and held the dustpan while I swept up the mess, and Nini put new peas in the vegetable dish.

That evening, after Holly and I had helped Nini with the birthday and tea dishes, we sat at the kitchen table drinking café au lait and eating bread soaked in cane syrup.

"You have a nice name," I said to Holly. "Like Christmas. I wish I had a name like that. How could anyone call a child Adelaide Aspasie?"

"You were named after someone, weren't you? Your mother?" Holly asked.

"My mother and some great-aunt or something like that. Isn't that dumb?"

"It's nice. Holly stands for Hollywood."

Nini sighed. "Your mother wanted to be a movie star!" she said.

Holly looked embarrassed so I asked, "Can you come with Nini next Saturday?" Saturday, the one perfect day of the week. No school, no catechism, no church, and no middle-of-the-day crazy Sunday dinner. "I have lots of movie magazines and we can have a picnic in the yard."

"I can come," she said. "I'll bring my stories."

"Now, Holly," Nini said, "I know them stories of yours! Don't you go filling Addie's head with nonsense about folks *you* don't know nothing about and things that ain't your business!"

"Oh, Nini, Addie will like the stories, and you know they're true!"

"I don't know no such thing! But I know whose business they ain't!"

"All right, all right. I won't bring the stories!"

But as I left the kitchen, Holly whispered, "Don't worry. I'll bring them."

I wasn't worried. But Nini had made me curious. The way she'd said they weren't Holly's business made me think they might be mine.

CHAPTER VII

SATURDAY BEGAN like the other six days of the week. Two orange-colored pills lay next to my dish of wrinkled stewed prunes.

"Good for what ails you," said Aunt Kate cheerfully on her way to the Joyful Mysteries.

"Eat the prunes before you get up from the table, Addie," said Aunt Eveline, folding her napkin into its initialed silver ring. "Before you go out to feed that dog."

"Tom fed her. I don't have to go out. He's got her in the park. See how easy it is to take care of Pumpkin? No trouble at all."

"And don't forget your cod-liver oil pills." There was

no distracting Aunt Eveline from what mattered. She followed Aunt Kate out of the dining room.

I stared at the prunes lying in their own brown juice. The problem was to get them down with a minimum of gagging.

The kitchen door swung open. "I'm here," said Holly, drops of rain sparkling in her dark hair. She took in the prune situation at a glance. "Get 'em down, Addie. Want me to go upstairs now?"

"No, wait for me," I said, taking a deep breath. In went a prune. Out came the seed. I didn't swallow. In went another. I spat the seed in the dish. I got all four slimy prunes in my mouth before I lifted my glass of ice water and washed them down before I could taste. I hardly gagged at all. The pills were easy and I stood up, the daily ordeal over.

Holly looked at me with admiration.

"Let's go," I said. We ran up the stairs and down the hall past the attic door.

"Where does that door go?" Holly asked.

"To the attic."

"What's up there?"

"The past," I said making a joke. "Old everything. Old clothes, old letters, old broken clocks, my mother's cedar chest, even Uncle Ben's old uniform and gas mask from the war, and somebody's Confederate sword — every single thing that was ever in this family and grew too old to live downstairs lives in the attic. It's all up there with the family ghosts!"

"What's in your mother's cedar chest?"

"Oh, nothing much," I said, surprised that Holly wanted to know.

"Let's go in the attic," Holly said.

"No!"

48

"Are you afraid?"

"A little," I admitted. "Oh, I help Aunt Eveline air the attic every spring and fall, but I don't like going up there alone, or with a friend."

"I'm not afraid," said Holly. "I live in the past."

I let that go by, but Holly kept up. "Let's go in the attic. Come on!"

"*No!* I won't go!" I said, surprised at my own vehemence.

"Oh, all right, then," Holly said, surprised, too.

Feeling suddenly awkward together, we went in my room. We sat down in chairs and began looking at magazines. Outside, the rain teemed down, making it so dark we had to turn a light on.

"Did you bring the stories?" I asked.

"Yes. I hid them in the kitchen. I'll get them later."

"Do you want to play something? I love Tarzan! You could be Tarzan and I'll be Jane," I said generously.

"I don't like Tarzan or Jane," Holly said.

"How about witches? I love casting spells. You could be —"

"No. That's baby. And, anyhow, I'm not that kind of witch."

"What kind of witch are you?" I asked, making another joke.

Silence while I tried to figure out what was wrong.

"What did you mean?" I asked.

"Do you want to hear about my other life?" Holly peered over the top of her magazine.

"In Chicago?"

"No. I mean the life I led a hundred and fifty years ago."

I smiled knowingly.

Holly looked down.

"All right. You can tell me about it," I said.

"I'm not going to tell you."

"Oh, come on!"

"No. You think I made it up."

"I don't think you made it up. Tell me."

"Are you positive you really believe?"

"Positive."

Holly sat down on the floor, crossed her legs, straightened her back by stretching her neck, and closed her eyes. She looked ridiculous.

"The Sagoma," she began dramatically, "squatted under the mango tree and gazed into the gourd. The goat bladder hanging in his ocher-matted hair was filled with spirits, and he switched the animal-tail whisk across the gourd, dusting evil away from truth." Holly slit her eyes to see how she was doing. Obviously she had memorized the whole thing out of a book. Satisfied with my expression, she continued, "Suddenly, he turned his bloodshot eyes on me and shouted in the guttural voice of his ancestor, 'You have been chosen! I see the snake! You will be a Sagoma!' "

Holly opened her eyes and looked at me.

"What's a Sagoma?" I asked.

"A witch doctor. I'm a witch doctor. I can see the future and the past!"

I couldn't think of a thing to say to that.

"It's true, you know. It's one of my stories, but it's true."

Another silence while I tried to make up a sincere remark. It took too long.

"I have to go now," Holly said coldly.

"Wait, Holly!" I cried, desperate to hang on to my new friend. "I have something to show you."

I took Edmond out of the secret *Photoplay* envelope

and handed him to Holly. I hoped she'd know what a big secret I was sharing with her, so I said, "No one's ever seen Edmond before." She didn't say anything, but she looked interested enough to stay, so I pulled out Jane Whitmore.

"She looks like you," Holly said.

"She does? It is me, really. I mean, I imagine myself being her, Jane Whitmore. It's my secret life. Like yours. Except," I added quickly, "mine is made up."

"Listen! I really did live a hundred and fifty years ago. I've put it all in stories and they're true. I'm going to put you in my stories, too."

"But my other life isn't true."

"It could be."

"Oh, no! And anyhow, if I thought it was, I might go around acting like Jane Whitmore and people would think I was crazy."

"What do you care? You made up Jane Whitmore; she's just as much you as Addie is, so you can act like either one."

"I have to act normal."

"What's normal?"

"Normal is obedient, well-mannered, and unpopular."

"Is that what you want to be?"

"No. But I don't see how you found out about your other life if you didn't make it up."

"I just concentrate on being in my other life. I told you — I'm a Sagoma."

"I bet! You can't do that."

"I can."

"How?"

"*Believe*. You've got to believe. Like church."

"Church doesn't have anything to do with that kind of believing."

"Yes, it does. If you believe hard enough, it's true."

"What if I try to believe?"

"You have to know."

"Okay. I know."

"You've got to be sure."

"I'm sure." I have the makings of a first-class hypocrite.

"Well, we'll try. But I don't know . . . if your faith isn't strong enough . . . meet me after lunch and we'll go to the attic."

"Why *there?*"

"Didn't you say the past was there? Your mother's things and all?" Holly looked at me in disgust. "If you're afraid, it won't work. After all, it's your own mother's things up there. You're not afraid of your own mother, are you?"

"No. Of course not!" What did my mother have to do with it?

"I have to help Nini now. After lunch."

Holly, the Sagoma, rose and marched off to the kitchen, leaving me wondering exactly what it was I was supposed to believe and be sure of, and why she was so interested in my mother.

Holly came back after lunch wearing a once-white silk scarf wrapped around her head like a turban. She had a thick, scruffy notebook and a feather duster, and whether by accident or not, flour was smeared across her nose. I realized she was supposed to look like a Sagoma and I had to cough to cover up a laugh. Ceremoniously, she led the way down the hall. I opened the attic door and we started up the steep stairs.

A funny feeling came over me; I almost expected to see my mother standing at the top of the stairs, dressed in white like her portrait. I was afraid to look, afraid she'd be there and afraid she wouldn't. I could almost hear Fifi yapping a silly bark at her heels as she turned quickly away.

"Come on," said Holly quietly, as though she, too, had heard. "Nothing can hurt you."

A memory comes back to me: I am very small and I have fallen and scraped my knee. Someone with quick gentle movements has washed and bandaged my knee, and holds me in her arms. She rocks me, and sings a song with the words:

Lindy, did you hear that mockingbird sing last night?
Oh, Lord, it was singing so sweet in the moonlight!
Singing round my cabin door . . . My little Lindy Lou!

The voice is sweet and true, but I can't see a face; I can only feel firm, round arms hugging me close.

"The first thing you have to do is concentrate," Holly said, breaking into my thoughts at the top of the stairs. We wove our way around old trunks, old chairs with broken caned seats, tables black with too many coats of varnish, an old grandfather clock that bonged slightly as we stepped over the loose floorboards. The rain beat on the roof and the wind whistled around the attic corner.

"This is my mother's cedar chest," I said.

"What's in it?" Holly asked, trying to open it.

"It's locked. Aunt Eveline has the key. Her portrait dress for one thing, and a Panama hat, I think. One she sent to Aunt Eveline that Aunt Eveline loves so much she won't wear."

"Do you think Aunt Eveline would give you the key?"

"Never. This chest is practically sacred. Even when we air the attic, Aunt Eveline won't let anyone help her with it."

"I'll bet there're some good things in there!"

"Like what?"

"Like love letters! Things like that."

"Maybe." If anyone was going to read my mother's love letters it was going to be me, not Holly. "But I can tell you, Aunt Eveline would never let us look inside."

"Oh, well, this is a good place to concentrate, anyway," Holly said, passing her feather duster over the chest like a wand. "I'll sit on this side and you sit on the other. Put your hands on the lid."

"Okay."

"Now, concentrate."

"On what?"

"On nothing."

"On nothing? How can I do that?"

"Pretend your brain is being washed clean. Empty."

"Okay. I can do that."

"Do it."

"I'm doing it."

"Now, let it fill with the spirit."

"What?" I felt foolish.

"Your other self. The one that was you in another life is filling you. That spirit is flowing into the clean, empty places. You are the other you!" Holly's voice wobbled dramatically.

I giggled.

"Now look," she said in disgust, "you ruined it."

"I couldn't help it. You sounded so fake."

"I am not fake. Listen, one day I was helping Ma cook. We were making Nini's chicken gumbo and just before the rich brown soup boiled, Ma turned off the fire and said, 'Add the filé.' For a second I was in another place stirring a pot and a voice said, 'Now add the asafetida,' and it was another time, and I was making a potion, and then, it flashed off. That was all the first time, but it was so real, I figured a way to add to it: every night from then on I concentrated, and I believed, and in the morning, I wrote stories about my other whole life!"

"But my secret life isn't like that. I make it up."

"It's another life. Maybe your mother's. Did you ever think of that? Maybe you were your mother before you were you!"

"That's crazy!"

"You've got to believe!"

I concentrated. "Nothing happens."

"Believe!"

I concentrated for all I was worth, empty, empty, empty. The light in the attic was failing. I felt tingly, peculiar. Something was going to happen. I waited — I was drifting away! I was — I was going to sleep.

"Holly," I said, snapping awake. "What are you scribbling?"

"I'm writing about your other life."

"You mean I was talking out loud?"

Holly was smiling her Sagoma smile. "No, you didn't talk out loud."

"Then how do you know what to write?"

Holly scribbled a few more words. "I know," she said maddeningly.

"Then tell me."

"You don't believe me but I'm a Sagoma. Even in my second life, I'm still a Sagoma. Next time when I come over, I'll have your secret life in stories for you."

The last thing I wanted was my secret life exposed to the public.

The rain had stopped and we could hear Nini calling. She wanted Holly to help with dinner. Holly jumped up and I caught a glimpse of her notebook, all lines and squiggles.

"Pure gobbledygook!" I said.

She was furious. "Only I can understand the stories!" She ripped the stained white scarf off her head and swatted the cedar chest with the duster as she turned away. "They are in a special code and I was going to teach it to you," she added, stomping past the bonging clock.

"I don't even want to learn it," I answered, following her. "And you've got flour on your nose."

"It's a *secret* code," she yelled, rubbing her nose angrily. "You couldn't possibly figure it out!"

"I'm sick of secret codes," I said, but I followed her all the way to the kitchen, where Nini put us to work chopping onions, garlic, and sweet peppers. Holly wouldn't speak to me as we chopped and chopped. Nini noticed the silence.

"Holly, you fillin' Addie's head with your nonsense?" Nini asked suspiciously.

"If you are referring to my stories," Holly said, "they are not nonsense, as *you* should know."

"Humph!" said Nini, chopping harder. She inspected what we'd done and ordered, "Finer!" and we chopped some more. I was wishing I hadn't told Holly about Edmond and Jane Whitmore.

CHAPTER VIII

⠦⠦⠦⠦⠦⠦⠦⠦⠦⠦⠦

"AUNT EVELINE," I said in my sweetest voice, "may I air the chest with my mother's things in it?"

I was helping air the attic for autumn. No matter that the thermometer still hit ninety degrees in the middle of the day, it was October, and if Aunt Eveline waited for a real "cool snap," she might find herself digging for the Christmas tree ornaments the same week she shook mothballs from our sweaters and wool skirts. When I was younger, I had thought Aunt Eveline made the cool weather happen. "Summer's over," she always announced. "We'll air the attic today, Addie," and sure enough, the next day when I put on my dark cottons, Aunt Kate would sniff a fresh breeze and say, "There's a definite touch of fall in the air this morning."

Aunt Eveline didn't stop sorting clothes as she answered me, "Thank you, dear, but I've already aired your dear mother's things and locked the chest." She held up a little key tied with blue ribbon and dropped it into her apron pocket.

"Could I just peek inside the chest, then?" I asked very meekly, looking longingly at her apron pocket.

"No, dear, we wouldn't want to expose darling Pasie's things to any unnecessary poking around. You may sort this pile of sweaters from Kate's chest. Some of them go clear back to the war!"

I looked at the heavy, dull-colored pile and wondered if she meant the Civil War. But I wasn't going to be sassy. I wanted to charm Aunt Eveline into giving me the key tied with blue ribbon.

We had divided the clothes into three stacks: one to put away for next spring, one for Aunt Kate to mend, and another to hang outside to air. I piled all Aunt Kate's things in the hang-outside stack, doing my best not to breathe. Nini had already washed the gauze curtains and the white linen slipcovers worn by the furniture in summer. Aunt Kate had mended them, and they were folded in attic chests, ready to be starched at the spring airing. The furniture downstairs was naked, scratchy, and dark, and the windows were smothered by a fringed kind of tapestry cloth that my grandfather had bought in Belgium.

I looked around the attic for something else that might have been my mother's. There was only the box of watercolor exercises I'd seen before. I thumbed through them. One was of the lagoon in Audubon Park, exactly the same view I had framed, only in this one, the colors were muddy and there was a swan drawn so badly it took me a minute to figure out what it was.

"Look, Aunt Eveline," I said, holding up the lagoon scene. "Terrible, isn't it?"

"Well, not terrible, but definitely still in the learning stage. She hadn't matured as an artist yet, Addie. As I told you."

"But this is worse than I do now! There's hope for me."

"Of course, dear. I've said all along: If you want to be an artist, I'm going to see to it you get the best training possible. Carry Kate's sweaters outside, please."

"Are you sure there's nothing in my mother's chest for outside?" I asked hopefully.

"Positive, dear. Come along now."

Defeated again, I trotted after Aunt Eveline, hugging the pile of dark sweaters, overpoweringly mothball, and itchy under my chin. "Aunt Eveline," I asked, gasping for clean air, "how did you start being an art teacher?"

Aunt Eveline stood still, wool skirts clasped to her bosom. "When I was quite small, I drew a portrait of Alphonse — he's that little china bulldog you play with, the one with the derby on. I drew him for Papa's birthday and Papa said, 'Eveline, you are a born artist!' And so, I knew I was! Everything Papa said was right." Aunt Eveline smiled, a remembering look on her face. "Your mother was the real artist, Addie. She would dress in something flowing, and with one of her beaux trailing behind her, carrying her paints and the picnic basket, she'd go to the park for a few hours and return with a landscape. She got the training she needed in Florence, and when she married and went to Honduras, she produced her mature work." Aunt Eveline sighed.

"And you, Aunt Eveline?"

"While I," Aunt Eveline laughed, "I outlined a plan of study for myself and I followed it. So many hours of anatomy, so many on color theory — I disciplined myself right out of any creativity that might have crept in. The trouble was, how could I, a lady, earn a living as an artist? And the truth was, someone had to earn money! But a lady? Why, I could teach, of course. It was the only work my father would hear of. So, now I can paint dog portraits that look exactly like dogs! Now, let's get these sweaters and skirts outside to air before the evening damp sets in."

I lingered behind, my thoughts on the future, the hours I would spend drawing live models and mixing paints from raw pigments, moving T-squares and triangles across the drawing board. I would do landscapes like my mother's, impressionistic watercolors that made you want to step into their soft greenness.

"Aunt Eveline," I called, "could you give me a few lessons now? Just to start?"

"Addie, child, that is what I'm trying to tell you. I'm not really an artist. Oh, I know the rules, but I might spoil your talent! Draw what you like now, and when you graduate from high school, you can go to a really fine art school to study."

I was about to answer when I smelled cloves. I shifted an old lavender sweater away from my nose, and a letter slipped out of the pocket. It was addressed to Aunt Kate in my mother's handwriting, and postmarked Florence, October 5, 1921.

"Aunt Eveline, may I stop for a while now? I have sort of a headache."

"You've done too much! Of course, do stop, dear. Lie down in your room. I'll bring you a lemonade with a little mint. Mint helps —"

"No, Aunt Eveline, I don't want a thing. It's not really a headache. I'm just a little tired." I escaped to my room to read the letter before Aunt Eveline could think up another remedy.

Dearest Katie, darling sister,

Here I am in "Bella Italia"! Can you believe it? Your own baby sister so far away? The sky is blue and cloudless, and the sun is bright — perfect weather. For days it has been so absolutely gorgeous, I hate to admit it, but I long for a good New Orleans rain. Darken, Heavens! Let the blue-black thunderheads batter the roof with their teeming rain, so loud I have to shout to hear my own voice! Oh, Katie, remember the day we found George's letters to Eveline and were reading them? (By the way, has he popped the question yet? What slowpokes they are!) That day the rain was coming down so hard on the roof, we didn't hear Eveline until she saw us. She was really angry, don't you think? Even though she just stood there, so pale.

I have started a diary, Katie darling, and you'll never guess where! I'll give you a hint: what is white and must be opened every day? You've guessed! Ah, but you won't be able to read it! It's in my secret code. No one can know my secret thoughts.

How is Fifi? Does she miss me?

How is — you know who? Pining away, he writes. He'd better. Was he "pining" at Mable's picnic? Did you go? Has Mable trapped Louis yet? *Write me!* Tell me *all*.

Katie, darling, I don't really like Florence much. I've tried but I still don't like it. All

61

those museums full of statues and old paintings. Do you think Eveline might let me come home at Christmas? Say a good word for me. I really can't paint a thing in this place. I don't even think I like to paint at all anymore, but don't tell Eveline *that*. Please, please, Kate dear, put in a good word for me. I shall die if I have to stay. I can hold out if she says I can come home for Christmas. *Try, try* for Christmas, Katie, darling.

Your loving little sister,
Pasie

It was as though my mother had come out of her portrait and was standing in front of me. Look, Addie, she was saying, I'm real — not the perfect princess of the portrait, and not Sandra Lee's mystery woman either. I'm a girl like you. She was calling me as clearly as if I'd heard her voice. I reread the letter.

She had been homesick and lonely, still far from being the artist she was to become. She had missed her little dog, and she had missed — you know who. Could that have been who she was looking at when her portrait was painted? And the part about Mable and Louis, Tom's parents — it didn't sound as though she'd liked Mable. Maybe none of it really mattered anymore to most people, but it did to me.

Aunt Eveline had forgotten the truth, if she'd ever known it, and Aunt Kate was too busy preparing for the next life to remember this one, but Aunt Toosie — she had been the sister closest to my mother in age. She would have known her best of all.

Since I was supposed to be recovering from a headache, I had to sneak out of my room. I took the shortcut

Sandra Lee and I had worn through the cherry laurel hedge.

Aunt Toosie was sitting at the sewing machine, her hands guiding soft green wool under the needle, her foot working the pedal, toe forward, heel back, toe forward.

"What was my mother like, Aunt Toosie?"

"Beautiful," Aunt Toosie answered, not breaking the rhythm. Heel back, toe forward.

"Everyone says that. And anyway, I can see it in the portrait. But besides — I mean, what was she *really* like?"

Aunt Toosie's foot stopped and she looked at me. "Addie, your mother was absolutely the most selfish person I have ever known. She thought only of herself. Maybe Eveline spoiled her and made her that way. I don't know. But I do know *she* spoiled Eveline's whole life. And do you know what? Everyone thought Pasie was so beautiful, but Eveline was beautiful, too. It was just that Eveline was so busy trying to take care of all us younger sisters and brothers, trying to run the house (with no help from Father, I might add), hold down a job . . . good heavens, she had no time for herself! If she'd dressed well and done her hair carefully, she'd have outshone most of the girls in town. As it was, George wanted to marry her."

"George who?"

"Your father! Didn't you know? Oh, Lord, I've said too much." Aunt Toosie looked flustered.

"*My* father wanted to marry *Aunt Eveline?*"

"Yes. He was Eveline's beau, much older than your mother."

"But — but —" I was speechless. "But how did it all happen?"

"Well, your mother was quite pretty, you know. With

very winning ways. I think she convinced your father that Eveline's health couldn't stand up in the tropics. And Eveline never denied Pasie anything — she just withdrew herself. She'd kill me for telling you this. But you *should* know it. You'd appreciate Eveline more if you'd lived with your mother longer." Aunt Toosie's toe and heel began to go to work as she turned back to the pretty material. "Go along now, Addie. I've gotten into a heap of trouble, I bet!"

I walked out of the house, stunned. My mother had suddenly turned into another person, the opposite of everything I'd always been told. What could have made my mother steal her own sister's beau? And how could Aunt Eveline forgive her, much less tell me she was a saint?

If I could get into my mother's cedar chest I might find clues, love letters, like Holly said. Aunt Eveline would never let me, but I could borrow the key. It was still in her apron pocket. Maybe *borrow* wasn't quite the right word. But Pasie was my own mother. They had no right to hide things about her from me.

Aunt Eveline was still dashing up and down the attic stairs, her curly hair damp around her flushed face.

"I feel much better now, Aunt Eveline," I said, scrambling back into bed just before she came into my room.

Aunt Eveline reached over to put her hand on my head, and there was the blue ribbon poking out of her pocket. I pulled it out the rest of the way and closed my hand on the key.

"Cool as a cucumber," she said.

"Why don't *you* rest awhile, Aunt Eveline?" I asked.

"I think I will," she answered, sitting down on the edge of my bed and fanning herself with the new *Photo-*

play. Her rosy cheeks and damp curls made her look young and different.

"You look pretty, Aunt Eveline," I said shyly.

"Why, Addie," she said, embarrassed, "I'm — I'm not pretty! No one ever thought so! At least, it's been a long time since . . . No, dear, I was never pretty. Your mother, now . . ."

CHAPTER IX

~~~~~~~~~~~~~~~~~~~~~~~~~~~~~~

IT WAS NOW OR NEVER. If I didn't get the key back before Aunt Eveline finished airing the attic, she'd miss it. I sat in my room pretending to do my homework, amazed at how much nerve I'd had stealing the key and how little of it was left now that I had to go into the attic. Alone. At night. Suppose my mother's spirit was guarding the chest? I'd been listening to Holly too much. I looked at the little key in my hand, and the thought of all the secrets the chest might hold banished my fears. I stood up, ready to sneak into the hall.

A tap on my door. Holly, the white scarf around her head and a Sagoma look on her face, walked in.

"I have a new story!" she said proudly. "Would you like to hear it?"

66

"Yes, I'd love to hear your story," I lied. The sooner she got it over with, the sooner she'd go home.

Holly stood up, chin high, notebook in her left hand, right hand ready for gestures.

"Jane Whitmore," she began, "was a young girl, beautiful and talented, and she loved a young man, handsome but dumb —"

"Now, listen, Holly —"

"Wait, Addie! This is true! — handsome but *dumb,* whose name was Edmond. Although Edmond loved Jane, he loved himself more and did not want to marry her, so —"

"Now, look here, Holly, that's *not* true! He does want to marry her. I don't want you meddling —"

"Will you listen? I am a Sagoma. I know. Edmond *never* marries! That's the whole trouble. Poor Jane never gets him. She —"

"I won't listen!" I put my fingers in my ears. "Holly," I said, calming down and speaking in the carefully modulated tone I use to make Aunt Eveline happy, "you've got to understand that this is *my* secret life. You don't have anything to do with it. It's *my* Jane Whitmore and *my* mother and I don't want you getting them mixed up like I know you're trying to do — for your own amusement!" I ended less modulated than I had intended.

"If you think my stories are about your mother, why don't you want to know about her?"

"I'll find out about her my own way! And I'll know a lot more as soon as I —" I caught myself before I said "as soon as I look in her cedar chest."

"As soon as you what?" Holly was instantly alert.

"Oh, nothing." I tried to make it casual.

"It's got something to do with your mother's chest! You've got the key!"

67

My eyes flew open in surprise. Was she really a Sagoma?

She laughed delightedly and said, "I told you I was a Sagoma! Let's go to the attic!"

"Wait a minute, now, Holly. It's *my* mother's cedar chest."

"You're going up in the attic *alone?* Where it's dark and scary even in the daytime?"

"Yes," I said weakly.

"You'll need me. It will be much better if there're two of us."

I started to give her more arguments, but I was beginning to think it might not be a bad idea — less scary and more fun. "Well," I said, "maybe, but we ought to wait until Aunt Eveline goes to bed."

"No, it's better now. She's busy in the kitchen, and I have to go soon." Holly opened my door.

I could hear Aunt Eveline talking to Nini, and Aunt Kate was bound to be in her room, working on the Sorrowful Mysteries. I should have paid more attention to the shadow that moved across the lighted hall, but Holly was already opening the attic door and I tiptoed quickly behind her.

"We can't use the light," I whispered, my hand on the switch.

"No," Holly whispered back, "they'd see us."

We groped our way up the stairs. "I know where things are," I said still whispering. "Hold on to me, and when we get to the chest, we'll just have to feel what's inside."

"And take what feels interesting to your room!" Holly said.

I was excited myself; I was sure we were on the verge of a great discovery.

At the top of the stairs, we turned left into the attic. A tiny bit of light came from the little outside window and from the hall door we'd left cracked open. The grandfather clock loomed over us like a black ghost, and the floorboards groaned under our feet.

"Here!" I said, reaching the chest. "I've got my finger in the keyhole!" I put the key in and turned the lock. The lid creaked open and the fresh smell of cedar flooded my nostrils. I reached in through soft layers of silk and cotton. I felt the stiff brim of the Panama hat Aunt Eveline loved, and groped for something interesting.

"Ah," whispered the Sagoma, both hands deep in rustling tissue paper. "I feel here the secrets of the past. I —"

I didn't have a chance to ask her what she meant. Everything happened at once: my hand closed on something cold and hard, the attic flooded with light, and footsteps pounded up the stairs.

Sandra Lee was in the lead, Aunt Eveline right behind her.

"I knew I heard someone in the attic!" Sandra Lee cried triumphantly.

Aunt Eveline took in the open chest and our guilty looks. "I'd almost rather have found a common thief!" she said, angrier than I'd ever seen her. "What are you doing?"

"We — we just wanted to see the portrait dress, Aunt Eveline," I lied.

"I'm sorry," Holly mumbled. "It was my fault for asking to see it," she added nobly, laying down her life for her friend.

"The key," Aunt Eveline demanded, holding out her hand.

I placed it on her flat palm.

"Adelaide, go to your room. I will mete out your punishment later. Holly, tell Nini what you have done. I am certain she will chastise you."

Chastise sounded even worse than meting out. I looked at Holly and felt sorry for my friend when I saw her face. I turned to Sandra Lee, concentrating as much hate into a glance as possible.

"What brought you here?" I said between my teeth.

"My homework," she said sweetly. "I needed the assignment." Even Sandra Lee looked subdued by Aunt Eveline's reaction.

Four unhappy people trooped down the steps. But all was not lost. In the pocket of my dress my hand was still closed over something hard and cold. I felt its shape with my fingers, and right then I knew what it was.

When we got to the bottom of the attic steps, I reached out with my left hand and tried to squeeze Holly's. I didn't think much about it at the time, but she was holding something close to her skirt. She managed a weak smile. I stole a glance at Aunt Eveline and knew I'd never done anything so wicked. I got into my room as quickly as possible.

For once, it was Aunt Eveline who shut the door. I took my hand out of my pocket. I was holding my mother's prayer book. The mother-of-pearl cover looked new, exactly as it did in her portrait. The cover was carved with a profile of Christ, and the spine of the book was strengthened with gold. It was locked tight by a gold clasp and there was no key. My fingers shook as I forced the lock and broke it open, showering a white, powdery dust in my lap. Something was funny about the pages — they were thick, and stiff, and starting to crumble. Then I saw that the Key of Heaven text had been painted over in white and the pages were full of small numbers in my mother's neat handwriting. It was "what was white and must be opened every day"! The numbers were the code she'd written Aunt Kate about. I'd found her diary! My mother's secret thoughts!

CHAPTER X

THE AFTERNOON AFTER we were caught, I stayed in my room alone with a tantalizing diary I couldn't even read. As if my secret life wasn't bad enough, my real life had become desperate. Aunt Eveline was cold to me and very polite. My punishment, she said (and she was right) was knowing I'd sinned. Holly had been banished from Three Twenty by Nini and Tom was at track every afternoon. I was supposed to take Pumpkin to the park every day, but I didn't feel like doing that. Now, it was almost time for Little Orphan Annie, and even Sandra Lee might have been better company than no one, but I'd scared her so much, she'd started listening to her own radio. I stared at the diary ready to rip the pages out. I needed help but I didn't want anyone else to read it.

I made up one good Jane Whitmore scene entitled The Ferry Boat Ride. In The Ferry Boat Ride, Edmond and I are crossing the river in the late afternoon, and he notices that the golden rays of the setting sun are not as golden as the soft curls that have escaped my hair ribbon and frame my face so charmingly. As he touches my cheek with trembling fingers, the sun sinks behind the earth, and I feel his passionate lips on mine.

Then, when I was all ready for The Proposal, the scene turned into a conversation between Edmond and me that went like this:

"Hurry, Jane! We'll miss the picnic!"

"Oh, Edmond, let's leave the others as soon as possible. There's a place by the lagoon I want to paint. The light will be just right early in the afternoon."

"But I want to show you off! You look lovely in that hat." He obviously adored me. He was about to propose, and I had already written my answer in my diary.

"I hear Mable and Louis are engaged!" I said.

"So she claims," Edmond answered.

"She has her ring and I think it's divine! I mean, it's a match made in Heaven, don't you think?"

"She's been carrying the torch for Louis long enough, I'll say that!"

"Edmond, that's mean."

"Well, Louis likes being a bachelor."

"Poor Louis, then. Only, I think he's a flat tire and he's lucky to have found someone who'll put up with him!"

"Jane! I thought you liked Louis! Listen, Jane, marriage is an institution, but marriage is love and love is blind, and therefore, marriage is an institution for the blind! Ha, ha! Get it?"

"Ha, ha. I get it. Straight out of last month's *College Humor!*"

"Jane, you wound me!"

"Let's go back. It's going to rain."

"Jane, you're not mad at me, are you?"

"No, of course not. Why should I be? Hurry. Let's go home."

Next door Sandra Lee was playing her phonograph so loud, it broke into my Jane Whitmore scene.

"I can't give you anything but love, Ba-by!" the voice on the record screamed. "Love's the only thing I'm thinking of, Ba-by!"

"Sandra Lee!" I shouted. "Turn that thing off!"

"Don't you like music?" she screamed back.

I looked across the short distance between our bedroom windows. Sandra Lee's golden curls shone like a halo around her head.

"I love *music!*" I hollered and slammed my window shut.

"Psst!" My door was open and there stood Holly. She slipped in and closed it carefully behind her. "I sneaked over," she said. "I *had* to know! Did you find anything? I didn't."

"I didn't either," I lied.

"Oh, well," said Holly, nonchalantly, "we'll just have to try again."

"Try again! Are you crazy? I wouldn't try again for anything! Besides, I don't have the key anymore."

"We can try my way," said the Sagoma.

I groaned as she took out her scarf.

"Listen! There's something going on! Can't you feel it? Don't you want to know what's happened?"

"What do you mean?"

74

"Just what I'm always telling you. If you can't feel it — a Sagoma *knows!* I know something. You have only to ask."

"I'm asking."

"You know what I mean!"

"I wouldn't dare go to the attic, if that's what you mean!"

"You have to dare! In this life," said the Sagoma, "to dare is to live!" She looked very pleased with herself. "Besides, I saw your Aunt Eveline leave for church."

"Aunt Eveline will kill us if she comes back and finds us," I said, but I was weakening. I could see that Holly was bursting to tell me something, and she was determined to do it her way. I wanted to know what it was. "Last time we were very unprofessional," I said. "We left the attic door cracked and I didn't pay enough attention to who might be in the house."

"No one's here now!" Holly said, wrapping the scarf around her head. "Let's go!"

We went carefully. I could still hear Sandra Lee's record, and Nini was singing "Keep the Homefires Burning" in the kitchen.

When we got to the cedar chest, Holly went through the usual mumbo-jumbo of dusting with the feather duster. We placed our hands on the lid and closed our eyes. After a short time, the silence began to fill with distant automobile horns and an occasional bird singing as it flew past the little attic window.

I sighed loudly.

"Shh!"

"Nothing's happening."

"Will you shut up?"

"That's not polite," I answered. "Aunt Eveline could

come back any minute. Nothing's happened. Nothing's going to happen."

"There!" Holly said triumphantly, standing up. On the lid where her hand had been was a snapshot in a little ivory frame.

"It appeared from nowhere!" Holly said.

"Holly, what is this?"

"It just appeared," she said stubbornly.

"You certainly don't expect me to swallow that!"

It was a snapshot of my mother with a man who was not my father. The man had dark hair parted slightly to the side and slicked down so flat, it looked lacquered. His face was in shadow, but I could see a mustache, and I could tell he was looking fondly at my mother.

He was terribly good-looking, wearing knickers and a bow tie. He looked like Edmond. My mother was looking straight at me, laughing.

"Holly! Where did you get it?" Even as I asked I knew she'd found it in my mother's chest. "You had to bring me all the way up here to give me this?"

She didn't answer. Looking very smug, she turned to leave.

"You got it in the chest, didn't you?" I yelled. "And you know who it is because Nini tells you things. And you put them in stories because you just love to pretend you're a Sagoma! That's why you're so interested in my mother!"

I felt triumphant until she shouted back. "Then that makes my stories true, doesn't it? Because if Nini tells me things, they're true. So there!"

"Addie?" Aunt Kate's wobbly voice floated up from the foot of the stairs. "Come down from the attic!"

We ran down the steps as fast as possible.

"What were you doing up there?" Aunt Kate asked in her querulous tone.

"Nothing." I knew Aunt Eveline would never have told her about my stealing the key.

"Do nothing in your room, then. Or better, say your beads." Aunt Kate touched my hair and her voice softened. "We have to take care of you," she said. "You're still our little girl."

I wanted to stamp my foot and scream, "I am not your little girl!" I mumbled it instead.

Aunt Kate, who is not always as deaf as she claims, heard part of what I'd mumbled, and said, "I remember when your mother said that! It was Christmas and she'd just come home from Florence. I remember . . ."

Aunt Kate smiled to herself and her voice trailed off after her memory. I escaped to my room with the ivory-framed snapshot.

JANE WHITMORE BACK HOME

A knock on the door.

"Kate!"

"Yes!"

"May I come in?" My golden hair, combed out, hung to my waist. I was wearing the nightgown Eveline had made for me; she had spent two whole days trimming it with Irish lace. In my hand I held my silver-backed hairbrush.

Kate smiled. She was sitting in bed, wrapping Christmas presents. I climbed up next to her and sat cross-legged. I began to brush my hair, conscious of the firelight playing on my curls.

"Thank you for talking Eveline into letting me come home," I said.

"How nice to have you home — my baby sister. Will you ever grow up, dear?"

I giggled. "Never. I will stay a little girl forever. At least,

Edmond seems to think so. Look at this snapshot Mable took of us. He's looking at me as though he thinks I'm just a child." Kate took the picture in her hands.

"Edmond is not going to grow up, either," said Kate in a different tone. "Youth becomes you, but it's high time Edmond amounted to something — and he never will."

"Oh, Kate! You don't know him. He's grown up, all right." I smiled to myself. "He's going to get his own apartment and he's going to write a book. Stories about the war."

"How can he write about the war when he didn't even go?"

"He did too! He may not have gone overseas, but he was in the army."

"The supply corps! In Atlanta. He didn't even leave the South!"

"He says his stories will be true. A definitive work about the South, and the war."

"If I know Edmond, they will not even be work, much less definitive."

I jumped off the bed. "You're mean, Kate!"

"Oh, darling," cried Kate, laughing. "You are the dearest child! Don't be mad at your old-maid sister! It's just that there are so many fine young men crazy about you. Why, look at Louis! He wouldn't marry Mable if he could have you. I just want you to be sure when you choose."

"I've chosen Edmond, Kate," I said quietly. "I hope you grow to like him." I turned and left Kate staring after me.

CHAPTER XI

~~~~~~~~~~~~~~~~~~

Y OU SAID YOU WERE COMING over to get *Lad Comes
Back*." Tom shoved the screen door open in his gen-
tlemanly manner and let it bang behind him. I had come
downstairs to find Holly and make her tell me who the
man in the snapshot was, and she had just informed me
that only in her Sagoma state could she possibly tell.

"I forgot about *Lad* whatever-it-is," I said carelessly.
I was too wrapped up in what was happening to worry
about a fictional dog. Edmond had turned into the only
man my mother had ever loved, the one in the snapshot.
He was on the tip of my mind the way words are sometimes on the tip of the tongue, and just out of reach.

"You forgot about Lad! I certainly hope you don't
forget about Pumpkin!"

"It was because my friend came over I forgot." I pointed at Holly, sulking on a kitchen stool. It was her first legal visit since Nini had chastised her. She glared at Tom and followed Nini into the dining room. Holly was very good at exits.

"She doesn't look very friendly."

"That's because she's mad at me."

"A great friendship." I ignored that and Tom continued, "Here's *Lad Comes Back* anyhow. You'll like it! In this one, Lad gets stolen and —"

"Don't tell me! I want to read it."

"Okay. I'm late for practice. *Please* don't forget to take Pumpkin out. I made the team and I'm going to pole-vault in the track meet next Saturday. I have to practice every day, even Sunday, and I need my sleep, so I can't go to dancing school Friday night. Isn't that great?"

The opposite of being asked for the contest in advance is finding out you won't even get half a dance the whole evening.

"Are you going?" Tom asked.

"Not if I can help it," I answered. I could just see Sandra Lee and Harold waltzing by Denise, Elizabeth, and yours sincerely, Adelaide Aspasie.

"Well, don't then." Tom kicked the screen door half open and crashed through, letting it slam behind him.

"That boy's manners are terrible!" said Aunt Eveline, coming into the kitchen as the screen door exploded against the doorframe. "Just because his father is not at home is no reason for Mable not to discipline him."

"Manners aren't important," I said. "It's sincerity that counts."

"My dear, manners are the expression of sincerity.

Good manners . . ." She was off again, but I wasn't listening. Tom had meant, was I going to the track meet, and I thought he'd meant dancing school.

"Tom!" I shouted out the back door.

"Ah-de-la-eed! Are you listening to me?"

Tom wasn't in sight.

Perfect Saturday. I'd made both Tom and Holly mad. I couldn't even find Holly, and Nini said she thought she'd gone home. The snapshot was as big a mystery as the diary. Nothing was right, in fact, everything was wrong, and the whole day was boring. I thought of going to track practice and explaining to Tom what I'd meant, but I couldn't do that in public. I was even ready to settle for Sandra Lee's presence, but when I went next door, I discovered she'd gone skating with dear Harold. As I was about to head back home, I overheard part of a conversation between Aunt Eveline, who'd come to borrow a cup of sugar, and Aunt Toosie:

"If there is an eleventh commandment," Aunt Eveline was saying, "it is 'Finish what you start,' as Papa used to admonish."

"Which is perhaps why he always made *you* start," said Aunt Toosie. "Sometimes when I think of what your life might have been if it hadn't been for Papa — and Pasie."

"Pasie? I count myself fortunate for having been like a mother to her!"

"Yes, of course, Eveline, but Papa ruled us like a czar and he made Pasie his czarina. Whatever they wanted, those two, they got, and they trampled you along the way, my dear. You know George would have —"

"I do not feel trampled, Toosie!" Aunt Eveline interrupted. "I am quite content. If only . . ."

I was sure she'd say, "If only my darling Pasie rested in Saint Louis #2," but she surprised me by saying, "If only I live to see Addie grown and happy!"

"Eveline! Of course you will! You're not sick, are you?" Aunt Toosie asked anxiously.

"No, Toosie, dear! But sometimes I feel — well, not exactly sick, but a bit tired. I feel as though I've led my life, and now, I only have to wait for Addie to grow up!"

I stood in the hallway until I heard Aunt Eveline leave through the back door.

"You were listening," Aunt Toosie said.

"I didn't mean to. Aunt Toosie, you don't think she's really sick, do you?"

"No dear. Just getting older."

"Aunt Eveline seems so different when she talks to you. With me she's — I can't tell what she's thinking. And she's strict."

"Oh, Addie, she doesn't mean to be that way with you! It's just that she changed after Pasie left for Belize. Your mother was like a daughter to her, a beloved daughter. There was almost a whole generation between them, you know, and they had different mothers because your grandfather married again after he was widowed."

"I know," I said, thinking that if Aunt Eveline was almost old enough to be my grandmother then my father had been old enough to be my grandfather!

"Eveline had such beautiful hair!" Aunt Toosie continued, "blond and thick, and she wore it in a French knot with little curls escaping around her face. So pretty!" There were tears in Aunt Toosie's eyes. "Then, after Pasie and George left, she cut her hair and just pushed it back with those ugly combs she still uses. She started wearing glasses, too. I think she did that, not to see better, but to hide her beautiful eyes." Aunt Toosie gave her nose a good blow.

"I'm sorry, Aunt Toosie," I said, not knowing what else to say. "Aunt Toosie, do you know who this is with my mother?" I showed her the picture Holly had found.

Aunt Toosie had to dab her eyes. Glancing carelessly at the picture, she said, "One of her beaux. She had so many."

"Yes, but who is this one?"

Aunt Toosie looked more carefully and laughed. "Well, it's not your father. He was much older and never wore anything but khaki as far as I can remember! You know, it's funny — it could be almost any young man of that time. They all looked alike in their knickers and slicked-down hair; they all looked rich, as though they had nothing to do but enjoy themselves. What a different world it was!"

As if to back up her statement, the doorbell rang and Aunt Toosie, peeking out from behind the organdy curtains, said, "Oh, Lord, another beggar!"

Happy days are supposed to be here again, but poor men, needing a shave and decent clothes, still ring our front doorbells. Aunt Eveline has a formula: if they ask for money, she refuses, but offers them a sandwich and milk on the back porch. If they refuse the food, they are not needy enough. Aunt Toosie's formula is far simpler: when she saw this dull-eyed, raggedy man, she tiptoed to the back without answering.

"They've got Eveline's number!" Aunt Toosie said, watching as the man shuffled down the walk. "Sandra Lee saw chalk arrows on the pavement pointing straight to Three Twenty, and look, he's going right over there!"

But he didn't turn in our walk. He just shuffled on.

I topped off this depressing Saturday alone in my

room. I fanned it clove-free, stared at the snapshot, worked on the code in my mother's diary, and flipped through *Lad* to read the ending first, something I'd never in my whole life done before. After supper, I slunk around the living room until Aunt Eveline's prying questions about how I felt,-and was I coming down with something, got me so mad, I said, "Yes, distemper," and was sent straight to bed.

CHAPTER XII

Sundays never vary.

"Hurry, Adelaide, we'll be late for mass!"

We are never late; we arrive at our regular pew and waste five minutes waiting for the eight-thirty mass to start. In the silence, broken only by soft footsteps hurrying, Aunt Kate's stomach rumbles loudly. I look at her to make sure no one thinks it is *my* stomach. Mass begins and I concentrate on my prayer book so Aunt Eveline will think I'm hard at work praying. Mass is over and I pull on Aunt Eveline's hand, trying to make her hurry, but she has something to say to everyone she ever knew. By the time I get home, I am so hungry even prunes are welcome. The morning is long and boring. Everyone I know stays in bed until time for eleven-thirty mass, so no one is around until one.

Dinner is at one. Aunt Toosie, Uncle Henry, and Sandra Lee hurry in at ten minutes after one. Aunt Kate sighs loudly and marches to the tureen of orange-colored soup. Thirty minutes later, we have finished the Jell-O, but the grown-ups linger over their demitasses, and Sandra Lee and I make our faces look as if we are thinking fascinating secret thoughts so engrossing we have forgotten each other's presence.

At three, the opera comes on the radio. Aunt Eveline tunes it up full blast so that she can listen as she putters in the garden outside. If it's one of Verdi's or Puccini's operas, she sings along, accompanied (after the Joyful Mysteries) by Aunt Kate.

"Mi chiamano Mimi!" sang the trio this Sunday. Mimi, Aunt Eveline, and Aunt Kate were dying of consumption and digging nasturtiums.

"Blah, blah, blah, blah," sang Sandra Lee, tone deaf and rude.

"Addie! Ad-die!" Tom hollered above the chorus.

"What?" I hollered back, leaping to the window. Aunt Eveline groaned. Tom and Pumpkin were standing in the nasturtiums and Tom had his skates on, but the groan was for my unladylike response.

I rephrased. "Yes, Tom?" I asked sweetly. "What is it that you wish to inquire about?"

"You have anything to do this afternoon?"

"Why?"

"I'm going skating in the park."

"I'm not allowed to do anything so foolhardy as put wheels under my feet," I replied for Aunt Eveline's benefit. She rose from the nasturtiums and marched into the house. "But I'll draw animals at the zoo while you skate!"

"I'll skate by the cages!" shouted Tom generously, as I grabbed my pad and pencil and ran out of the room.

"I figured out what you meant yesterday," Tom said when I came out on the porch. "I thought you didn't want to go to the track meet, but you meant you didn't want to go to dancing school."

"A brilliant deduction," I said.

Tom grinned sheepishly. "So long, Pumpkin." He patted Pumpkin on the head and we put her in the shed and walked to the zoo. Tom carried his skates and hung around while I started sketching.

"Aunt Eveline says that when you draw animals, you should draw their movement," I explained to Tom. "You're not supposed to outline. Think of the muscle *in* the lion's thigh and show it move the leg."

I tried to remember as I drew. Tom skated around the cages and in the side street. Every once in a while, he'd skate up behind me and watch some more. "Pretty good," he said. "Not bad."

After I'd finished a lion and a few monkeys, Tom came back. "When I left home, my mother had gingerbread in the oven. It ought to be done by now. That's a nice monkey you did there."

"I'll come home with you," I said, closing my drawing pad.

We cornered Aunt Mable as she opened the oven door. She cut two thick slices of hot gingerbread while Tom shook the cream into the milk and filled our glasses. We went outside, and, balancing the milk glasses on the plate of gingerbread and taking turns holding it, we climbed the oak tree by Tom's window to a place where the trunk forks. We sat there munching the gingerbread and washing it down with milk.

"Tom! Tom! Where are ya, boy?" Uncle Malvern's voice was thick and fuzzy.

"Don't answer," Tom said to me. "He won't come looking and I don't want to see him."

"Tom! Don't be mean!"

"I can't stand him."

"He's not so bad. No worse than Aunt Kate."

"What's wrong with Aunt Kate? She doesn't drink."

"She smells of cloves. She's old."

"That's not her fault! What's so bad about being old?"

"I don't know. Nothing really. Only I wish . . ."

"What do you wish?"

"I wish I had my mother. Instead of Aunt Kate and Aunt Eveline. My mother'd still be young and pretty. Like other mothers."

"Aunt Eveline's pretty! In an old way, maybe, but I like the way she looks."

"She looks okay. But you don't understand. It's awful to have an old guardian, not even a real mother. All the other girls have modern mothers and I have — two old ladies dressed in lavender."

"That's not nice of you, Addie!" Tom was genuinely surprised.

"Sandra Lee makes fun of Aunt Eveline's old-maid ways. And I have absolutely no confidence in her methods of bringing me up!"

"Yeah. Look what a mess she's made so far!" said the great comedian.

"Ha, ha. So terribly funny." How would Jane Whitmore get out of a tree with dignity? I tossed my head, and dropped the piece of gingerbread I needed to finish off my milk.

"There y'ar!" Uncle Malvern's triumphant voice boomed under our dangling feet. "Whatcha up to?" He was lurching back and forth and leering up at us.

"We're not up to anything, Uncle Malvern," Tom said angrily. "What do you want?"

"The wheels," Uncle Malvern said, slurring the word as though it had a *j* after the *l*. "The wheels stuck."

"Come on, Addie," Tom said to me. "He means the wheels of his perpetual motion machine. I'll fix them, Uncle Malvern."

Tom jumped down without looking back at me. He kicked open the screen door and took the hall steps three at a time. When I caught up, he was standing in Uncle Malvern's room. There, in the middle of the floor, was a card table piled high with the perpetual motion machine. An old erector set connected wheels and more wheels, including a bicycle one. There were tubes, milk bottles, and a battery with loose wires hanging over the edge of the table.

Uncle Malvern huffed and puffed up the stairs. "Won't go!" he said between wheezes.

"It's not connected," Tom said. "Pulled loose."

"Supposed to go by itself," said Uncle Malvern sadly. " 'Petual motion."

"You don't suppose you really invented such a thing, do you?" Tom asked mercilessly. He screwed the wires to the battery.

The wheels squeaked and turned, air bubbled out of a tube into the water-filled milk bottle and rose to the surface in gurgles. A drumstick among the turning wheels beat a rhythm as steady as a heart on Tom's old toy drum.

Uncle Malvern clapped his hands, happy as a small

child with a wind-up toy. "Lookit that boy go!" he said.

Tom was halfway down the steps before he shouted back, "Come on, Addie! Let's get out of here!"

We got out of the house quicker than we'd come in.

"Tom, you're really mean to your uncle!" I said, panting.

"Listen, Addie. He deserves it. He doesn't do anything, even for himself. My mother has to do it all."

"I'm sorry, Tom. Aunt Mable doesn't seem to mind, and I don't see why you have to be *that* mean."

"Well, how do you think you are to Aunt Eveline? And she loves you. She does everything for you."

"I'm not mean to her! I love her! Really."

"You didn't sound like it a minute ago."

"She's all right. I didn't mean I don't love her."

"Funny way you have of showing it, then. I don't think you love her — or anybody else!"

"Now, listen, Tom!"

Before we could get into a real fight he said, "I have to help my mother with supper. So long."

"What a martyr!" I called after him. On the way home I tried to figure out exactly how I did feel about Aunt Eveline. I decided love didn't have much to do with how nice people were to you. Look at how much Aunt Eveline had done for my mother; if my mother had loved her back, she wouldn't have married my father. She'd stolen my father from Aunt Eveline to spite the man she really loved. She must have done it with what Aunt Toosie called her "winning ways."

THE WINNING WAYS OF JANE WHITMORE

"Fifi! Fifi, come along now, you silly dog! You'll spoil your new ribbon."

With Edmond's hand under my elbow, I stepped daintily

around the puddle. Edmond carried my watercolors. The light in the park was clear after the rain. Drops clung to the Spanish moss so that it hung weighted from the oaks and sparkled like daytime fireflies. The gazebo was washed snowy white.

"Paint those ducks," cried Edmond, pointing to a duck family paddling around the smooth lagoon.

"No, I prefer that." I pointed to a swan gliding across the water in front of a dark green background. "Yes, that!" I cried, reaching for my watercolors.

Edmond spread a small mat on the damp earth and we sat close together, not speaking, while I began to sketch. I tried to remember what I'd learned in Florence: Look within, not at outlines.

Edmond chuckled.

"What's funny?" I asked absently.

"Your swan looks like a pot with a long handle," he said.

I stabbed the paper with my pencil, snapping the point.

"Jane! What's the matter?"

"A pot with a handle!"

"I didn't mean —"

"You *did* mean! You *are* mean!"

I didn't bother to pick up my things. "Come, Fifi!" I stumbled over the roots of a tree and stepped in a puddle, hurrying to get away.

Edmond was picking up scattered brushes and pencils. "Don't go! Wait, Jane!"

Wait. I was always waiting for Edmond. For ages we'd been going to parties together and everyone assumed we were engaged, but he'd never progressed beyond deep sighs and hand holding, while I waited.

Edmond caught up with me. "Jane, darling, I was joking! You know I love your watercolors."

I stopped and looked him full in the face. I wanted to make my voice firm. "I don't ever want to see you again!" wobbled my voice.

He stood staring after me as I stomped off toward home, tears blinding my sight, and Fifi, her new ribbon muddy and bedraggled, yapping at my heels and begging to be picked up. I was through waiting for Edmond. There were other fish in the sea. One was sitting in the porch swing when I got home.

"Hello, George," I said.

"Hello, Jane."

"Where's Eveline?"

"Doing dishes. She said to wait here for her."

I sat down on the narrow porch swing next to George. He started to get up.

"I don't bite," I said, laughing at him.

Too large for the swing, he had to put his arm in back of me. George blushed, smiled, and settled down, terrified. This was the man who faced wild animals in the jungles of Central America.

"Tell me about Honduras and the banana plantation, George," I said.

"It's primitive and fascinating."

"What are the people like?"

"Mostly Indians, friendly, good workers, if you lead them. I enjoy the work. Of course, the climate is harsh, too harsh for anyone as young and delicate as you." George smiled and touched my hair with one finger. Noticing the beads of perspiration on my forehead, he added, "You'd melt." Pause. "And you're so young. Eveline might be strong enough."

"Eveline *strong?*" I cried, amazement in my voice.

"Isn't Eveline healthy?"

"The climate would kill her," I said.

"Kill her?"

"The heat. She doesn't talk about it, doesn't want anyone to know — she's really very brave — but she has — she has dangerously high blood pressure."

"I didn't know!" George murmured, stricken, absently still playing with one of my curls.

"Oh. Hello." Eveline walked out on the porch, drying her hands on her apron.

"Eveline!" George leaped to his feet, blushing furiously.

When I finished that scene, I rushed to my *Photoplay* envelope and snatched Jane Whitmore out. I was about to tear her up, but I couldn't do it. Instead, I tore Edmond to little bits. Then I cried. I'd never again draw anything so beautiful as Edmond Hilary de St. Denis.

CHAPTER XIII

ON FRIDAY I got sick. It was easy. I didn't try to swallow the prunes. I ate them slowly. When I came to the fourth and last, I let it slide down my throat. It came back up, bringing the first three with it. I knew by Aunt Eveline's look that I had escaped Friday night dancing school.

"I'm not dying, Aunt Eveline," I finally managed to say.

"Of course not, dear, of course not! To bed immediately! No school for you and no dancing school!"

That done, I had to give the appearance of regaining complete health by Saturday morning so that I could watch Tom at the track meet. It didn't work.

"Foolhardy!" Aunt Eveline cried when I wanted to get up the next day. "You have to recuperate!"

I had just convinced her that I could recuperate as well at the track meet when Holly came.

"Why don't you come back after lunch?" I said to Holly. "I have to go somewhere this morning."

She looked at me carefully. "I have to go somewhere this afternoon," she said.

"Can't you go in the morning?"

"No."

Pause.

"I wrote a story for you. Shall I read it?"

"By all means," I answered. My sarcasm was always lost on Holly.

"I've used Jane Whitmore, of course."

"Of course."

"It takes place when your mother — I mean, Jane, has returned home after studying in Italy. Listen! It's called 'The Scarves.' " Holly cleared her throat and read:

"Jane Whitmore had just gotten back from Florence looking as gorgeous as ever. One afternoon, she was downtown shopping for Christmas presents when she saw George, looking lost, wandering around a counter full of scarves, a saleslady behind him, looking impatient. Jane walked over to him.

" 'George,' she said softly, watching him jump.

" 'Oh! Oh, hello, Jane. I was trying to find something for Eveline. They all look alike.' He picked up a scarf and looked at Jane helplessly.

" 'How's this one, George?' Jane asked, tying a white silk scarf over her hair so that just a few curls peeped out. She was standing close to him and looked up shyly.

" 'You — that's a lovely scarf, Jane!' he said.

" 'Now, isn't that a perfect scarf, sir?' the saleslady said. 'The young lady does look sweet.'

" 'Yes, perfect,' George said. 'I'll take it — and the grey one there. Wrap them as gifts, please. Separately.' George smiled down at Jane."

Holly looked at me. "The end," she said.

"Jane wouldn't have done that!" I said. I opened my mouth to say more and burst into tears instead.

Holly turned motherly. "Now, that's good for you," she said. "Cry it all out, Addie!"

I ran upstairs and threw myself on the bed. By the time I'd pulled myself together, I'd missed the track meet and there wasn't enough left of the morning to do anything. Aunt Eveline took in my puffy red eyes and nose, and suggested that sunshine might further my recuperation, and would Holly and I like a picnic in the yard?

"How jolly!" I said, but was ignored by Holly and Aunt Eveline. Aunt Eveline made a big show of slicing cold chicken, stuffing eggs, and packing the picnic basket. We trooped out for a grand total of twenty feet and spread the checked picnic cloth, and ate in silence. After lunch we sat on the grass making clover chains and being polite to each other.

"Harold beat Tom!" Sandra Lee shrieked. She was in such a hurry to tell me, she started yelling halfway down the block.

"So what?" I yelled back, tearing the clover chain to pieces.

"Please," said Aunt Eveline, rocking and fanning herself on the front porch, "don't let me hear that expression. It's common."

Nothing about Sandra Lee and "it's rude to shriek at people half a mile away."

"Sandra Lee," I said with quiet dignity, now that she stood panting over me, "if Harold beat Tom, it means nothing to me."

"It was so exciting! Tom had the school record until today! Then, Harold jumped a whole inch higher!"

"Tom and Harold do not *jump,* they *pole-vault.*"

"Now, Addie, don't be disagreeable over a technicality," Aunt Eveline butted in. "Sandra Lee has been sweet enough to run over and tell you the news and . . ."

It was too much. I marched into the house.

"Harold asked me for every contest for the next three weeks!" Sandra Lee shouted after me.

I gave Sandra Lee and Holly enough time to get sick of Aunt Eveline and go away, then I sneaked down the back steps and over to Tom's house. I threw a small handful of gravel at his window.

Tom came to the window. "You're supposed to throw pebbles at *closed* windows," he said.

He took the shortcut through the oak tree to the ground. He was carrying a book called *Wild Animals I Have Known.*

"I'm sorry Harold beat you, Tom."

"He didn't beat me. He pole-vaulted higher and beat the school record."

"Well, I'm sorry about that, then."

"Don't be sorry. He just pole-vaulted higher. What's there to be sorry for?"

"I didn't mean — I mean — I wish you'd won."

"Let's just stop talking about it, huh? Why didn't you show up at the track meet?"

"My friend came over again."

"I'm sick of that friend. Not much school spirit either."

"You don't have to get mad. I was sick besides. I'm only trying to be nice."

"If you can't *be* nice, don't *try*. It ruins it." Tom's freckles were turning dark.

"What ruins what?" I asked, fascinated.

"If you're not sincere, if you have to try. That ruins it."

"I am extremely sincere. I came here just to tell you how sorry I am you lost the track meet."

I counted four very dark freckles sprinkled in the shape of the Big Dipper across Tom's nose. His cheekbones stood out and his lips were thin.

"Yeah, you really knocked yourself out. You couldn't make the track meet, but you came all the way next door. Here's a book I like," he said with an effort, tossing it to me and turning on his heel in an exit worthy of Edmond.

I would have enjoyed the scene more if, before Tom went inside, I'd thought up the line, "Tom, what a trying fellow you are!" Still, it was a pretty good scene, for real life. I went home, fixed a lemonade to go with the lace cookies Nini had just baked, and went out on the porch to enjoy my full recuperation and try out a new code on the diary.

CHAPTER XIV

❧❧❧❧❧❧❧❧❧❧

THE NEXT DAY began like every other one, with Aunt Eveline coming into my room to wake me up. But this time she was holding herself more stiffly than ever. She was dressed up more than usual, and around her neck she wore the grey silk scarf saved for special occasions. Her hair was pulled back in her no-nonsense way, and the plain tortoiseshell combs she wore to trap her curls were so firmly planted on either side of her head that she gave the impression of having been recently scalped.

"Addie, dear, Aunt Kate has passed on."

It took me a minute to catch on, to remember that in this family no one dies; they go to their reward, depart this vale of tears, or pass on to eternal rest, with, of course, the all important stopover at Saint Louis #2. Aunt Eveline was saying that Aunt Kate had died! I felt a little thrill of fear.

"I'm sorry, Aunt Eveline," I said; but I was thinking, I'll be rid of the cloves; and then, what is wrong with me? Aunt Kate has *died*. Adelaide Aspasie, don't you care about *anything?*

". . . her heart . . . in her sleep." I was barely listening. I'm not normal, not even sorry when my own aunt dies. I don't love my own aunt! I'm not even sure I love my own mother. Lord, make me love somebody! I managed one small tear that wouldn't even spill, and then a fearful thought: Do I love *Him?* Aunt Eveline had stopped talking, with her voice going up at the end in a question I hadn't heard.

"I'm sorry, Aunt Eveline. What did you say?"

"I said, Addie, that when you have finished eating your prunes, you and Sandra Lee are going with Aunt Toosie to Saint Louis #2 to make sure the cleaning men have done everything they are supposed to do and the place is ready."

This was Aunt Eveline's delicate way of saying we were to make sure Uncle Ben was no longer there; to see to it that when the cleaning men opened the tomb, they burned what was left of the wooden casket so that it would fall through the grill to the earth below, along with Uncle Ben's bones.

"I am staying with Kate, of course, and . . ."

I didn't hear the rest. Staying with Kate — staying with a body — a dead person. I couldn't wait to leave. I ate my prunes, gagging worse than ever, because at that moment the florist brought in a blanket of oversweet lilies, smelling heavy enough to hide even cloves.

"Now, Toosie," Aunt Eveline said, as Sandra Lee and Aunt Toosie, both crying buckets, appeared in the hall. "You'll have to wear gloves, and something suitable, Toosie, dear. That yellow linen you have on has no sleeves. How about the lavender polka-dotted dress and jacket hanging in my armoire? The size is indeterminate and fits anyone. And you, Addie, may carry my bag and pay the cleaning men, how much do you think, Toosie, I'm sure five dollars is more than enough?" On and on as though no one had sense. "And make sure there are no weeds; the tomb was freshly whitewashed when Ben moved in, so that's no problem, but it's truly a worry about Ben, it's so soon, you know, and the men may not do the right thing."

As far as I could tell, Aunt Eveline had not shed one tear. Of course, she knew Aunt Kate was going straight to Heaven, since Aunt Kate had made the Nine First Fridays when she was only eight, and had worn out goodness knows how many rosaries since then. But didn't Aunt Eveline feel sad? It didn't show. Aunt Kate was moving on, and all of Aunt Eveline's concern seemed to be over the next stop.

Finally, the three of us escaped, Aunt Toosie draped in lavender polka dots, and me trying to keep Aunt Eveline's enormous handbag from bumping against my knees. Sandra Lee skipped all the way to the Avenue, where we caught the streetcar. We paid our seven cents each and marched to the front for a long side seat, slightly ashamed that we might enjoy ourselves. It was nice to rock along Saint Charles Avenue, a breeze coming in the window, while Aunt Toosie remembered out loud who'd lived in which houses when she was growing up.

I felt guilty that no one seemed to care much that Aunt Kate had died. I hoped people would cry buckets over me when my time came. Dear, dear, Addie! What a loss to the world — a great talent cut off in its prime! I was so moved, tears came to my eyes. When Sandra Lee looked at me, I smiled bravely through the tears, knowing she thought I was crying for Aunt Kate.

The streetcar clanged its way around Lee Circle, with General Lee on his pedestal facing "the North he'd never turned his back on," according to Aunt Eveline. Aunt Toosie said she felt like a girl again, on her way to Canal Street to meet a friend under the clock at Holmes. Then she saw my tears and brave smile, and, sighing, sat quietly until we transferred to the Canal Street car. We rode as far as Claiborne and walked the rest of the way to Conti Street and Saint Louis #2.

Some people call it "the City of the Dead," and it does look like a little town with small, white stucco houses, all closed in by high walls. The walls are really vaults, stacked three high, where poor people have been buried. They are called ovens, because on the inside of the cemetery wall, small doors for caskets are oven-size. In places, the plaster has fallen away and the brick shows through, with ferns growing in the cracks. It's as though someone felt sorry for the scarred walls and planted fern to hide the neglect.

We passed the few trees and walked down the path between the little houses that stood crowded together, leaning toward each other like old friends. They were separated sometimes by a plot of weeds where long ago one had given up and tumbled down. Some tomb-houses were big and had iron grille fences forming small yards in front, but ours was small and boxlike and stood alone at a drunken angle. No one could remember when the marble slab with our name on it had been broken and lost, exposing the roughly plastered, over-size door, but the rest of the tomb was whole and, thanks to Aunt Eveline, covered with snow-white paint.

Aunt Toosie stepped carefully through high weeds, brushing fuzzy seeds off the polka dots as she wove her way between some neglected tombs toward ours. We followed single file. Even with the sun out and the sky bright, there was a stillness that made us intruders, guests calling at the houses of the dead. I stayed close behind Aunt Toosie, so close that when she let out a little cry and stopped suddenly, Sandra Lee and I ran into her back like actors in a comedy. I looked up to see what had startled her. There in front of us was our tomb. And in front of the tomb was — Uncle Ben! I recognized his grey pin-striped suit, the stiff-collared shirt, and the very tie Aunt Toosie had given him for Christmas! Missing were his chiseled features and his white, slightly drooping mustache stained with orange soup. Of course, he was lying down in his open, wooden coffin, but I thought I saw the front of his suit rise in a breath. Next, he would sit up and make his perennial joke, "Hi, there, Toosie-Woosie! You're not a floosie, are you?" Aunt Toosie gasped, and as though her breath set air in motion, a soft sigh of a breeze passed over Uncle Ben and his clothes began to vanish, suit, shirt, tie, leaving, oh horrors, only what was left of Uncle Ben himself. I stared, glued to the ground, as the breeze blew dust around a skeleton. Aunt Toosie and Sandra Lee were screaming, and the workmen Aunt Eveline had hired to clean the tomb came hurrying over.

"Ah, miss, don't take on! You shouldn't have come. We were taking care of this."

But Aunt Toosie and Sandra Lee turned and ran,

dropping gloves in the weeds, tripping over stones, while I stood completely transfixed. There on the ground just inside the mouth of the tomb, almost covered by a few bones, lay something — something I recognized. I took a deep breath, walked over to it, grabbed it, and ran after the others. Panting, I caught up with Aunt Toosie and Sandra Lee at the gate.

"Ben," Aunt Toosie said feebly. "The bones . . ." She turned quickly toward Canal Street and the streetcar, and we followed breathlessly. The streetcar was coming, its wheels clacking crazily: The hip bone's connected to the — thigh bone . . . them bones, them bones, them — *dry* bones . . . *hear* the word of the Lord!

We ran to meet the car, climbed on, and fell into seats. The thing I'd found was like a presence hiding in Aunt Eveline's bag, almost as frightening as seeing Uncle Ben's speedy departure. The streetcar rocked gently, the breeze soothed, and the lullaby wheels now repeated only the last line of "Dry Bones." I tried not to think about Uncle Ben.

Suddenly, I noticed we were going in the wrong direction. We had boarded the car heading away from the river and the old part of town. We were going toward the lake. I realized Aunt Toosie had done it on purpose when the car arrived at Metairie Cemetery. There was the towering Moriarty tomb with its four life-size female figures Aunt Eveline called "Faith, Hope, Charity, and Mrs. Moriarty." Aunt Toosie marched purposefully to the door. Sandra Lee and I had all we could do to follow her out, across the street, and into the cemetery office.

By the time we got home, Aunt Toosie had collected herself, all except the gloves. "We can't," she told Aunt

Eveline. "Kate just can't go to Saint Louis #2. The place isn't ready."

"Isn't ready? Didn't the men come?"

"Eveline, he's still there! Ben is still there!"

"How still there? How much of him?"

"Eveline, for God's sake! The cleaning men had already opened the tomb and taken the coffin out and — and Ben was still — was still a *skeleton!*"

"But if it's just the bones, the men will burn the casket, and the bones will drop through the grill to the bottom, making space for Kate, and . . ."

"Eveline, stop! I've already done it. I took the streetcar to Metairie. I've talked to the people in the office there. I put my name, the *family* name, in the contract. We have a plot in Metairie."

Aunt Eveline sat down. "We have a plot? Under the ground? You intend for Katie to move into a strange place? Under the ground?"

"Aune Eveline, it's not fair to Uncle Ben!" I said. "There's no room for Aunt Kate right now unless . . . it's not fair."

Aunt Eveline's straight back curved. Parts of her face drooped. Her hands twisted the grey silk scarf at her neck. In a moment, she might fall apart like Uncle Ben. But the moment passed, and she turned her blue eyes on Aunt Toosie. "Toosie, you are bohemian! How can we — but — what can I do? I suppose — I suppose it's not as bad as not even knowing where Pasie is."

Aunt Eveline put her hands in front of her face. I couldn't tell whether her tears were for Aunt Kate, my mother, or Aunt Toosie's bohemian ways, but it was the only time I ever saw Aunt Eveline weep. Sandra Lee had disappeared into her house the minute we got home, and

I found myself crying with Aunt Eveline, real tears at last. I cried because I couldn't stand to see her cry, and I cried because the thing I'd found in the tomb was the gold heart my mother had on in the portrait. I was afraid to know what it was doing in Saint Louis #2.

CHAPTER XV

AUNT EVELINE MADE Sandra Lee and me kneel by the open coffin in the living room to say a prayer for Aunt Kate's soul. I watched Sandra Lee cast her eyes down to her folded hands, her yellow curls hiding her face. I made myself look in the coffin. Aunt Kate lay under a blanket of death lilies with just enough of her showing to catch the waxlike hands clutching her worn rosary. I stared at the hands so as not to look at the face. Then, forgetting to pray, I jumped up.

Tom had walked in with Aunt Mable and Uncle Malvern and stood by me until we had to leave for church.

The hardest part was over, and the rest went like a bad dream. They closed the coffin, and we climbed into long, black cars and followed Aunt Kate in her even longer black car, first to church for mass, and then to

Metairie. Aunt Eveline sat very straight and stared ahead. Sandra Lee and Aunt Toosie sniffed and blew.

I took Aunt Eveline's cold hand and she clasped mine and did not let go until after Aunt Kate had been lowered into a hole dug in the ground, too dry for floating, and, it seemed to me, too firm for even spiritual escape. I felt my first real pity, if not love, for Aunt Kate. I thought that even tidal waves were better than that hole, and the little white house in Saint Louis #2, where my whole family rested together, was cozy by comparison.

When we got back home there was practically a party, with neighbors, friends, and cousins, and Nini going nearly crazy serving coffee and little sandwiches. Finally, everyone left and Aunt Eveline went to her room. I went to mine and took out the little gold heart I'd found at Saint Louis #2.

There was no doubt about it, it was my mother's. Even the links of the chain, alternating square and round, were just like those in the portrait. The chain was clasped closed, as though a neck had been inside it. I shivered and decided it was time to get some help with the code.

I went next door. Aunt Toosie and Sandra Lee were doing dishes, and I helped them until Sandra Lee went upstairs. Then I said, "Aunt Toosie, look at this."

"Why, it's Pasie's prayer book!" Aunt Toosie took it in her hands. "Where did you find it?"

"In the attic. Look inside. The prayer pages are painted over and it's all in numbers. Mother wrote them."

"What utter nonsense! And just like her. What is it supposed to be? Some kind of code?"

"Yes, it's her diary. I thought maybe you knew about the code."

"She wouldn't have told *me*. How typical — ruining

her beautiful book just to be different. Exactly like when she chopped her hair off only days before her wedding — to show off, of course! Who'd care about reading her diary, anyway?"

"I would."

"Oh, darling, of course you would! How ugly of me! I'm so sorry. Sometimes Pasie still has the power to get my goat. But listen, dear, I *did* love her. She was irresistible, really. That pretty face and gorgeous hair! Even after she cut it she looked adorable. I'm just jealous, still! Isn't that silly?"

I tried a new tack.

"Aunt Toosie, if all of Mother's things are either in the chest or lost in the hurricane, why was her gold heart in Saint Louis #2? Because that's where I found it." I produced the heart.

Aunt Toosie turned pale. "It couldn't be," she whispered. "She always wore that heart, and she was lost in the hurricane, everything in the house with her." Aunt Toosie took a deep breath and said with conviction, "You must be mistaken."

"I picked it up by the tomb, right after you ran away. From underneath Uncle Ben."

"Oh, Addie!" Aunt Toosie shivered. "You are like Pasie! Daring — and unafraid!"

"Yes, and I'm going to break the code in her diary!" Aunt Toosie was staring at me.

"I don't think she's daring," said Sandra Lee, who, with her usual sense of timing, had come downstairs again. "I think she's nosy. Miss Butinsky herself. If your mother wrote in code she didn't want you to know what she said, and it's none of your business."

"It is too! After people die you can read their letters. It's perfectly all right after they die!"

"Not if they didn't want you to know!"

"She did want me to know. She still does! I can tell. And it's *my* mother!"

"Thank goodness! I wouldn't want a mother with secrets. I wouldn't want a mother who had a boyfriend that wasn't my father."

"*Sandra Lee!* Go to your room! You are punished!" Aunt Toosie was practically screaming and her hand trembled as she pointed to the door. "*Your room*, young lady!" I'd never seen her angry with Sandra Lee before. She turned to me. "Addie, dear, run home. I apologize for Sandra Lee. Don't bother Eveline with this. I apologize . . ."

"But, Aunt Toosie, you didn't say how you think the heart got there if all of my mother's things were lost in the Gulf. And — and who was my mother's boyfriend?"

"Your mother had many beaux *before* she was married," Aunt Toosie said nervously, "and she probably left her gold heart at Three Twenty when she went to Honduras. She left many things she didn't think she'd need. Like her portrait dress. And — and someone put the heart in the tomb in remembrance of her, you know. One of the times the tomb was open."

Aunt Toosie looked pleased with these complicated explanations and, like all grown-ups, when she made up her mind something was true, evidence to the contrary didn't change it.

I went home. It would have been a waste of time to argue with her.

JANE WHITMORE PACKS FOR BELIZE

"*Your hair!* What have you done with your hair?" Eveline wailed. Her eyes were round, and tears were forming. "Oh, my God, Jane, what have you done?"

"It's not such a tragedy. I've cut it." I was busy packing my trunk.

"It looks adorable." Edmond had come into the room and was looking at me sadly. "You look like an adorable little boy."

My hair, chopped off two inches from my head, formed a curly halo around my face.

"Your veil won't fit! We'll have to do the whole crown over," Eveline said.

"I'm not wearing it. I'm not going up the aisle dripping lace and covered over like a cot with a mosquito net. I'm going to wear my going-away suit, and we'll be married in the sacristy."

"The sacristy! You won't fit. I mean the guests won't fit in that small room!"

"My sisters will. I don't care about the rest," I said, folding my portrait dress carefully.

Edmond laughed uncomfortably. "May a very old friend squeeze into your heart and into the sacristy with your sisters, Jane?"

"Since you think marriage is an institution for the blind, I thought you'd prefer not to see the ceremony. Ha, ha. Get it?"

"Jane! Run along, Edmond, it's bridal jitters. All brides act this way, I'm told." Eveline took a deep breath and turned back to me. "Now, dear, we can't change our plans at this late date. Of course, I'll alter the crown to fit, but the guests are invited. The curls around your face are — are endearing! You're just overwrought! Have you talked to George?"

"George and I don't talk. When we're together, he makes sure someone else is there too. George doesn't want to be alone with me."

"Jane! What nonsense! George asked you to marry him!"

"No, I asked him. And he was afraid to refuse. Oh, Eveline, how can you be such a hypocrite? Everyone knows you wanted to marry George. Unfortunately, they also know George wanted to marry you. Even George knows that but he's too dumb to do anything about it."

Eveline's eyes were dark holes in her white face. "That will be quite enough, Jane!" she said as George walked in.

"Pack only what you need," George said the minute he saw my portrait dress hanging in the trunk. "And don't bring jewelry," he added, looking at the gold heart hanging around my neck. "The climate mildews clothes, and it's better not to have anything valuable in the house."

Eveline began taking my beautiful dress out of the trunk.

"I want all of my things," I said, snatching it from her and stuffing it back into the trunk. "Everything."

George sighed and did not answer.

"Now, Jane, darling," Eveline said, "do as George suggests. Where could you possibly wear your portrait dress in Honduras, dear? And I'll keep your jewelry safe for you, dear! Don't forget, you are going to a banana plantation, practically in the wilderness!"

"Eveline! I don't want to go! I'll die! I know it!"

"Jane!" Eveline looked horrified. "George will take care of you. George — " Eveline turned to George — "don't worry. She's so young, and she's always loved her home. I'm afraid I've protected her too much, but she'll grow up." George stood silently looking at Eveline. "She'll love it, I'm sure. Just think: the tropics, the palms, the natives!" Eveline warmed to her subject. "Think of the glorious colors she can paint!"

"Eveline!" George moved closer to her. "Oh, my God, Eveline . . ."

Eveline gasped at the look on his face and rushed out of the room. George stood staring after her, and I stuffed my gold heart into my suitcase without his noticing.

CHAPTER XVI

HOLLY HELPED NINI every afternoon during the week of the funeral. I helped, too. Nini noticed we weren't speaking and finally said, "My, my, so busy helping, no time for relaxing! My, my, what good, sweet girls!" I giggled and Holly grinned. We had made up.

"Holly," I said as sweetly as I could when Nini left the kitchen for a minute, "please tell me who the man in the snapshot is."

"Offhand, I am unable to say," said Holly coolly. She looked me straight in the eye. I know a dare when I see one.

"I believe you are a Sagoma, Holly," I said, concentrating on my most sincere look. "Who is he?"

"Not just like that!" she said.

I smiled encouragingly, like the hypocrite I am. "Let's go to the attic."

We went, careful not to creak any more than we had to. My mother was waiting for us. I tried to make myself believe it was my imagination, but she did everything short of materializing. She wanted me to understand her; I was sure of it. I felt as though the three of us, Pasie, Holly, and I were in a conspiracy against the rest of the family.

Holly began. "Sit still," she told me. "Put your hands on the lid."

"Holly," I whispered, "I feel like my mother is here. Her hands are on the lid, too, and she's laughing!"

"Hush, will you? It's working, of course. Keep your eyes closed."

Holly closed her eyes and began to mumble. I kept my eyes slit open. Holly looked so silly, I was sure Pasie would giggle.

"Are your eyes closed?" Holly asked.

"Yes," I said, closing them.

"Aspasie!" Holly drew the name out in a wobbly singsong. "Aspasie, we are calling you! Are you there?"

A tap and a giggle. I think it was my giggle, but I had not tapped.

"Aspasie! We are waiting. Are you there?"

I could feel a sneeze coming on. I tried to hold it back. I was listening hard. She was going to speak. I squeezed my eyes closed; I was sure I'd see her if I opened them. It was working. If only I didn't sneeze. In a last-ditch effort to keep from sneezing, I brought my hand up from the lid to put my finger under my nose, but midway up, my hand collided with Holly's arm, and all at one time, I sneezed, opened my eyes, and someone said, "Ma!"

"Addie, you ruined it! She's gone."

She was, giggling all the way.

"She was about to tell us something," said Holly in disgust. "Can't you control your animal instincts?"

"There's nothing animal about a sneeze. I had to sneeze. She made me sneeze just then. I'm sure of it."

Holly looked at me. "At least you know it's starting to work, don't you?"

I thought a minute. "Yes," I answered. "She said 'Ma!' She was trying to say she was my mother."

"You see! I told you I was a Sagoma! If you hadn't sneezed, she would have finished telling you out loud what she whispered to me."

"She didn't whisper to you!"

"She did too!"

"What did she whisper? Did she say who was in the snapshot?" I played right into her hands.

Holly took her time. She was making up her mind how much information to feed me.

"She didn't exactly say that." Holly had decided to hold out. "She said she couldn't reveal to us at this time who the man in the snapshot was."

I lost my patience. "Then, that's exactly what she told *me* before I sneezed — nothing!"

"You can take it or leave it," Holly said in a very un-Sagoma-like tone.

"I'll leave it," I answered. "I *am* leaving."

My exit was spoiled by the fact that I had to go quietly, and could not storm out. Holly was tiptoeing along behind me. At the foot of the steps, just before we opened the hall door, she hissed at me, "How do you suppose I came by her white scarf?" She waved her Sagoma scarf under my nose. "It got thrown out, that's how, and Nini saved it. Look at the saltwater stains on it!"

Something terrible happened inside me. I felt my head drain. I tasted salt water on my lips. For a second, I thought I was remembering something, then it flashed off. I followed Holly all the way downstairs, unable to speak.

In the living room sat Sandra Lee, glued to the radio, her golden head bent over her paper and pencil. Little Orphan Annie had just finished her latest adventure, and Sandra Lee was poised for the code.

Holly tried to slam the swinging door as she went through the dining room to the kitchen.

"Shhh!" Sandra Lee frowned.

I laughed shakily. "That's so baby," I said. "Who cares what they have to say that's so secret? It's probably: 'Drink Ovaltine, dear little members of the Secret Society, and you'll get round, and pudgy, and all the boys will love you!'"

"It is not." Sandra Lee looked at me scornfully. "And if I were as skinny as you, I'd drink as much Ovaltine as possible, no matter who said what."

"'Beauty is in the eye of the beholder,'" I snapped, not having the faintest idea what that meant, my thoughts still on the white scarf.

"Beauty may be in your eye, but it's nowhere else," retorted Sandra Lee, knowing exactly what she meant.

"All right, boys and girls, gather closer!" said Uncle Andy, the announcer. "Is your *brand new* 1937 secret message decoder pin ready? Remember, now, nobody but 1937 members will be able to understand the *exciting* secret message, so if you haven't been a faithful member of the Secret Society, Little Orphan Annie wants *you* to tell your *mother* right away to go out and get you some *Ovaltine* so you won t be an *Outsider*. All you have to do is send us a foil seal from the can and ten cents and we'll forward you *your very own badge* and booklet and make you a *full-fledged* member of Little Orphan Annie's Secret Society! Ready now? Here we go: This is the seven-A secret code! Twenty-fourteen-A . . ."

I watched Sandra Lee write. Uncle Andy was calling out numbers and Sandra Lee was jotting them down with spaces between some. I stood absolutely still. Over the radio, the theme song was coming to a close: "Who's that little chatterbox? . . . It's Little Orphan Annie!" Sandra Lee was spinning the dial on the pin and writing letters above the numbers. The letters formed words, just as the numbers in my mother's diary might if I had a Secret Society decoding badge. Of course! I'd borrow Sandra Lee's.

I walked into the kitchen in a daze. Nini looked at me in a funny way and said, "Holly's gone, honey. She burst out of here fit to be tied. You all sure can fight!" I went upstairs. There was something about the scarf buried in the back of my mind. It was something I didn't want to remember. I grabbed *Lad, a Dog* and read straight through to the end.

The next afternoon I ran all the way home from school to beat Sandra Lee. Aunt Toosie was in her kitchen, but she was singing "Tiptoe through the Tulips" so loudly that I was able to get past her and up the stairs without being heard.

Too bad Harold couldn't see Sandra Lee's room. What a mess! I went straight to her ruffled dressing table. It was so beautiful with its little gold-framed mirror, glass top for showing off snapshots of friends, and a small, shaded lamp. But the ruffles were smeared with lipstick, and a knotted hair ribbon trailed in an open box of powder. Straight pins, bobby pins, and rubber bands spilled out of a silver dish. Half buried in the dish was Little Orphan Annie's Secret Society badge. I snatched it up and hurried out past Aunt Toosie, who was still tiptoeing at the top of her lungs. As I headed up the steps of Three Twenty, I could hear Sandra Lee calling good-bye to Harold, who had carried her books home for her.

I tried every combination I could think of, spinning the dial and trying to make letters fit numbers. Nothing made words. At five-thirty, Sandra Lee went screaming around her house looking for her precious badge. I couldn't risk trying to put it back on her dressing table, so I decided I'd better plant it somewhere here. I tucked it between the cushions of the chair she always sat in and watched her find it just in time for the five-forty-five Little Orphan Annie broadcast.

CHAPTER XVII

After school the next day, Tom walked in balancing a plate of pralines in one hand. Aunt Eveline and Aunt Mable were always baking things for each other, and this particular plate had been traveling between Three Twenty and Tom's house so long no one knew whose plate it really was.

"Tom," I said, using both hands to take the pralines, and making a decision. "Do you think you could decipher a code?"

Tom helped himself to the praline with the most pecans. "Probably," he said.

I took the second-best one and told him about the diary and how I'd found it, and then about the heart and how brave I'd been picking it up.

"It was lying there under Uncle Ben's skull," I said, stretching the truth a little because Tom was so obviously impressed. "And I snatched it out and ran for all I was worth!"

"I could figure this out," he said, looking at the diary. "It looks easy. But it's private."

"It's private all right, but that doesn't matter. She's dead and doesn't care."

"How do you know she doesn't care?"

"I just know."

"Why do you care, then?"

"Well, she was my mother."

"Oh."

"Will you do it?"

"I guess so. Give it to me for a day. Let me have another one of those things," he said, still eating the last praline he'd taken.

"Addie! Ah-de-la-eed!"

"I've got to help Aunt Eveline straighten Aunt Kate's room. I'll get the diary back tomorrow. I'm coming, Aunt Eveline!" I shouted, rearranging the plate to cover the bare spots.

No one had disturbed anything in Aunt Kate's room since the funeral. It was just as she had left it except for the dust Nini banished daily. Aunt Eveline had decided to air Kate's room, so at least the window was open when I walked in.

The walls were papered in a faded blue floral design, and the old mahogany furniture gleamed richly under an English wax applied monthly by the joint team of Nini and Aunt Eveline. The potpourri of brown rose petals and black cloves sat on a doily in the center of Aunt Kate's mirror-topped chifforobe, a small idol ruling over the silver-backed set of hand mirror, comb, and brush, and the painted tin box that held the souvenirs Aunt Kate had saved. The only thing that spoke of Aunt Kate's absence was the crocheted bedspread, which lay too smooth on the bed. The thick smell of cloves had been saving up for me; I could hardly stand it, in spite of the open window.

"We will leave it exactly as she did," said Aunt Eveline, with finality. "We will give her clothes to Nini for the church, but we will leave the room *just as it is*. Addie, why are you holding your nose in that ugly manner?"

"The cloves," I said nasally, breathing through my mouth. "Please, Aunt Eveline. Can't we throw out the potpourri?"

"Addie! Aunt Kate made that potpourri with her own hands! She dried the rose leaves and followed directions out of the *Ladies' Home Journal* exactly."

"It stinks," I said, "all the way into my room."

"Adelaide, if ever I hear you use that word again . . ."

"What word?"

"I can't say it. And please remove your fingers from your nose."

"I can't. I'll throw up. You mean stinks?"

"Adelaide!"

"It stinks, and there is no other word."

"Adelaide, go to your room!"

I did, but not without looking hard at Aunt Kate's box of souvenirs on her chifforobe.

I waited in my room until Aunt Eveline went downstairs, and then I sneaked back to Kate's room and got the box. It was painted black and on the top were her initials, KWW, in gold letters. It was so full of things she had saved that when I opened it, they fell out: letters, holy medals, newspaper clippings, a pale golden curl tied with white ribbon in an envelope marked "Aspasie, '06." My mother would have been a baby.

Mostly there were letters, but I saw only one envelope addressed to Aunt Kate in my mother's handwriting. It was postmarked Belize and dated before I was born. Someone had painted a black border around the edge in imitation of a death announcement. The only thing in it was a New Orleans newspaper clipping from the society section that read:

ASPASIE WOODS MARRIES
GEORGE LATHROP AGNEW

Then:

The little edifice was decorated beautifully with palms and Easter lilies about the chancel, and with numerous candles and electric lights for the high noon wedding mass of Miss Aspasie Woods and Mr. George Lathrop Agnew. The bride was given away by her brother, Benjamin; her only attendant was her sister, Marie Louise ("Toosie" to her friends). The bride was striking in a lovely gown of duchess satin trimmed with duchess lace, and worn with a long veil of illusion and lace held with a crown of orange blossoms from which the bride's own short curls escaped, framing her lovely face in the latest fashion.

The strains of "Melody in F" and "The Lullaby from Jocelyn" were delicately played on the violin, as well as other appropriate melodies, as the handsome pair became man

and wife. Mendelssohn's Wedding March re-
sounded on the organ as the bridal party left
the church for a small reception at the bride's
home at Three Twenty Audubon Street. The
bride's sister, Miss Eveline Woods, was
dressed in tan canton crepe trimmed in lace,
as she received her guests in the artistically
decorated house with quantities of pink roses.
Miss Katherine Woods, another sister of the
bride, assisted Miss Eveline.

After the reception, the bridal pair left for
a honeymoon cruise aboard the S.S. *Managua,*
which will take them to Honduras and their
new home.

At the bottom of the clipping, handwritten by my
mother in the same black ink used on the border of the
envelope, was a mock announcement: "Here lies Aspasie
Woods Agnew," with a thick black arrow pointing to the
word *Honduras* in the clipping.

Poor Pasie! She'd been unhappy from the very beginning. But how could she have expected anything else
when she hadn't loved my father, and she hadn't wanted
to leave Three Twenty? She'd done it all to get even
with the man she really loved. I was sure he was the one
in the snapshot and that Aunt Eveline knew him, but I
couldn't show her the picture without admitting that
Holly and I had helped ourselves to my mother's things.
I didn't want Aunt Eveline to know any more bad things
about me.

I returned Aunt Kate's box to its place on her dresser
and went downstairs to the kitchen. After I'd apologized
to Aunt Eveline for saying stink, I asked her if my
mother had liked Honduras.

"Even better than Florence!" Aunt Eveline said. *"How* she loved that glorious country! She wrote so often begging us to visit!"

"Why didn't you go, Aunt Eveline?"

"Oh, well — I always intended to — I was terribly busy at the time. But some of their young friends visited them, and then, of course, they had many friends in Honduras. Your mother especially loved the two young natives who worked for her, Lola and Sussanah, their names were. What a delightful life she had in Honduras!"

I couldn't tell if Aunt Eveline had fooled herself or if my mother had succeeded in fooling her, but I was sure that if I could read the diary, I'd know.

Tom returned the diary the next day at school. He'd wrapped it in a brown paper bag.

"I couldn't do it," he said, handing it to me as the bell rang. "I don't think you can either. It's not a real system, you see. No one could figure it out."

"She *said* it was a code! My mother said so."

"Not really. It's impossible to decipher by logical methods," he said in a stuffy, irritating way.

We had to hurry to get in line before we marched into the classroom. After the Pledge of Allegiance and morning prayers Sister Elizabeth Anne told us to open our geography books.

I had known Tom didn't want to decipher the code from the first. Of course it was logical. He just hadn't tried. I looked at the diary again as I was slipping it under my geography book and noticed that three numbers, 1, 15, and 26, were repeated over and over; something I hadn't seen before. I worked with them, trying out "who," "the," "and." Then I noticed another group of numbers, 20–23–20–23, repeated twice on one page, and right in the middle of Sister Elizabeth Anne's lesson on the products of Brazil, it dawned on me — if 20 was F, then 21 was G, 22 was H, and *23 was I!* I'd broken the code! 20–23–20–23 made — "Fifi!" I shouted.

The whole class turned around and laughed, except Sandra Lee, who said loud enough for me to hear, "Just like Aunt Kate!"

Sister Elizabeth Anne rapped on her desk for order, and her one eye that did not look toward Heaven (I discovered right then and there it was her left) bored into me. "Adelaide," she said, "we are not in need of a court jester. For your punishment you may write the Eight Beatitudes eight times each, while the rest of the class has recess."

The bell rang and everyone except Sister Elizabeth Anne and me hurried to the courtyard.

"Blessed are the poor in spirit," I began, and as I wrote, I thought: When I get home, I'll figure out the whole entire diary! There can't be anything wrong about reading someone else's secrets as long as they're dead. "Blessed are the meek," I continued. And it's my own mother, after all. She wouldn't mind. It's not as though Holly or someone not related to her was reading her secrets. "Blessed are they that mourn." It would be nice, though, if Holly could do it with me. Not that I'd let her read anything *really* personal. But Holly's worked hard digging into the past and —

"Adelaide, continue writing, please."

"Blessed are they that hunger and thirst after justice." And it would only be just to share it with Holly. We could really have fun — she would make it better, in her Sagoma way.

"Blessed are the clean of heart." We could go to the attic for a little atmosphere.

"Adelaide!"

"Blessed are the merciful." I owe it to her. I'll invite Holly to help me decipher the code!

"Adelaide, recess has ended!"

"Blessed are they that suffer persecution for justice's sake, for theirs is the kingdom of Heaven," I scribbled for the eighth time.

CHAPTER XVIII

T HE MINUTE SCHOOL was over, I ran home with nothing on my mind but the diary. I tore into the kitchen, and there was Holly, drying the dishes Nini had washed. She didn't turn her head or say hello when I came in.

"You'll rub the design off the plate," I said in an offer of friendship.

No answer.

"Holly? I'm sorry about what I said."

"Sagomas learn to bear with lack of faith."

"It wasn't that I didn't believe, really. I was just upset. I hate not remembering my mother for myself."

"It's funny you don't remember before you were six. I do."

"What do you remember?"

"Everything. I remember my Daddy. And my Mama."

"What about them?"

"Everything. The fights especially. They couldn't think the same thing about anything, and they never shut up. And while they talked angry, the babies cried."

"What babies?"

"There was always a baby. I have two little sisters and one little brother."

It was the most Holly had ever said about her life in Chicago. While she talked, she seemed like a different person. Now, she went back to being Holly: "If I weren't a Sagoma, I'd go crazy. Maybe you're lucky you don't remember."

"My mother and father didn't argue," I said, suddenly remembering that. "I remember silence. Long silences when no one talked." I remembered two people sitting at a table, the click of their forks as they ate and didn't look at each other. I remembered fear because of the silence. "Sing!" I'd cried to the woman. "Sing Lindy Lou and the mockin' bird!" The man stared at me, and the woman who was Pasie, of course, jumped up from the table and ran away awkwardly because she had on very high heels and was absurdly dressed in something long and flowing. Absurd because the man, George, wore khakis and was dressed for the jungle, which was where they were.

"Holly!" I said. "I do remember parts!"

"Of course you do. You've only forgotten because you didn't want to remember. It's all there and you'll remember more if you believe. I'll put it all in the stories."

"Holly!" I said. "Guess what? I have the diary!"

"What diary?" said the Sagoma, suddenly alert.

I told her about the prayer book, so excited that I kept jumping ahead of my story. "We can decipher the code together!" I finished.

"A Sagoma never refuses help to someone in need," she said, laughing and hanging the dish towel on a hook. "Let's see it." Holly led the way to my room.

I handed her the prayer book and she took it as though it were the Holy Grail.

"It's gorgeous," she said, sighing and passing her finger over the carved mother-of-pearl. "Full of secrets!"

I had a moment's doubt. "Maybe I should start alone and then —"

"No! We have to start right away. I feel it!"

"Okay," I said, back in the mood. "Let's go to the attic for the right atmosphere!"

"How about the cemetery?"

"The cemetery! Why there?"

"It's where you found the gold heart, isn't it? We'll bring the prayer book and put it where the heart was, and Pasie's spirit will be drawn to it and she will help us interpret the diary!" said Holly dramatically.

It did sound better than the attic.

We told Aunt Eveline the truth — almost. We said we were going to the cemetery to bring a dahlia in memory of all those who rested there. We had found a lone dahlia in the yard, still holding on to part of its late summer color.

Aunt Eveline gave us about a dozen rules and regulations about getting to the cemetery, but she was so delighted that I was doing something for "darling Pasie" that we finally got away.

I took two sharpened pencils and a notebook for the deciphering. We could start with a key matching the whole alphabet with numbers. We'd have the diary read in nothing flat.

"Are you going in *that?*" I asked, when Holly appeared on the sidewalk. She had dressed in a long skirt with a new scarf wrapped around her head. She looked ridiculous, like a gypsy or a nut. Thank goodness Sandra Lee was at the dentist and didn't see us.

"If my native dress embarrasses you, you may walk behind me," she said.

"Oh, no, nothing like that," I said, but I dropped back now and then to tie my shoelace.

It was one of the three summer days that Aunt Eveline says always come in October. By the time we got to Saint Louis #2 on the streetcar, the temperature was in the high eighties, and thunderclouds were forming on the horizon. Holly walked slightly ahead of me. She has a nice walk. I tried to match the slow swing of her hips, but that's very difficult if it's not clear where your waist ends and your hips begin.

We tramped through the weeds to the tomb, following the path in back of the main aisle. The tomb had a new rough cement covering over the hole Uncle Ben had recently reentered.

"Put the prayer book exactly where you found the heart," Holly said.

"I can't. It was sort of inside with the bones, and now the opening's sealed."

"Close to the opening, then." Holly pulled my mother's scarf out of her pocket and wrapped the book in it.

"Stop!" I was shivering. She put the little white package against the mouth of the tomb.

"Don't you want your mother near while we work on the diary?"

"I guess so," I said. It was a strange way to begin, but there was no way to stop Holly going through the usual ritual. In the background of my concentration I could hear the thunder growing louder. Clouds came over the sun and the sweat on my head turned cool.

"Aspasie! Are you there?" called Holly. Her voice wobbled beautifully.

Lightning flashed, timely and dramatic.

"Oh, God," I whispered.

"Hush. Speak to us, Aspasie!"

"What the dickens are you girls doing there?" The caretaker was scratching his head and staring at the Sagoma in her native dress. "Get inside my lodge. You won't have time to go anywhere else before the rain hits. I feel a drop now!"

It had to be one of the most mortifying moments in my life. I looked at Holly. She was not mortified, she was livid with rage. She grabbed my hand and mumbled, "Let's get out of here!" We took off like jackrabbits, but not in time to beat the rain. Before we'd gone ten feet, it came in torrents, heavy and opaque, beating us with its fury.

"Here!" Holly shouted, pulling me against a large tomb-house. We pressed ourselves against the front wall, away from the rain falling in sheets from the overhang. I pushed as far back as I could — and felt the wall give slightly! Holly had been leaning back, too. She stumbled as the marble entrance slab, large as a door, scraped open a crack!

We looked at each other, wide-eyed. My heart sounded louder than the rain. Holly shoved, and the crack opened wider. We could see a gloomy, cobwebbed interior. Holly pushed until the opening was large enough to slip through.

"Let's go in," Holly said in a low voice.

"You first," I whispered back. Lightning split the sky, with a loud clap of thunder right behind. "The prayer book!" I hollered, suddenly remembering, and without stopping to see if Holly understood, I raced back. The rain was coming to an end as quickly as it had begun, and was over by the time I reached our tomb.

There in a puddle lay a soggy little bundle. I picked it up and the scarf fell apart in my hands. The mother-of-pearl sparkled like new as the sun came out, but inside, the painted pages were soaked sticky, and the numbers smeared to grey blobs.

How could I possibly have forgotten it? I wanted to die! The most important thing in my life — destroyed! I I moaned out loud, hugging the diary to my heart. Miserable and wretched, I wandered back to the tomb where I'd left Holly.

"Holly!" I wailed. "Look at my book!"

There was no answer.

"Holly?"

Silence.

Was she *in* the tomb? I gathered my courage and looked through the crack. I waited for my eyes to adjust to the dim interior. I saw a carved stone casket, the kind used to hold wooden coffins. Sitting bolt upright on the floor, hands rigid on the casket, eyes closed, was Holly, pretending to be in a trance. I had to admire her nerve.

"Enter!" commanded the Sagoma without opening her eyes. "You are invited to view a scene from the past! Enter!"

The smell of the tomb-house was musty, the smell of death and decay. I stumbled into the vault, conking my head on the low ceiling.

"Be seated! Place your hands on the casket! Close your eyes!" came the command.

The stone floor was cold and moldy. A spiderweb brushed across my face and tangled in my fingers. When I opened my mouth to say something, I hiccuped.

"Holly, the diary. It —"

"*Pa-sie!*" called the Sagoma in a ringing voice. "Tell us what is troubling you! We have traveled back to meet you! We are spiraling into the past!"

I felt dizzy. I heard the rustle of a skirt and a giggle.

"Yes, Pasie!" Holly said excitedly. "I see it! I understand! I —"

"You understand what?" My eyes were open, staring at Holly who was staring at me.

"I understand everything now! Did you see it too?" she asked.

"See what?"

"A wooden coffin! The kind of wood they use in the tropics."

"No, I didn't see a thing."

"Around the coffin stood three mourners, their faces in shadow. 'Whose coffin is this, Pasie?' I called."

"I didn't hear you call anything."

Holly ignored me. "The answer came back as though played on an old phonograph — scratchy, echoing: 'Mi — ine!' "

"But she didn't have a coffin! They didn't find —"

"Do you want to hear the rest?" Holly asked.

"Of course," I said hastily.

" 'Who are the mourners?' I called out. 'Ba — en! Lou — iss! Ma — all — vern!' she answered, stringing the *l*'s out into space as she left!" Holly paused and waited for me to say something.

"How could you hear all that in that short time, and I didn't hear any of it?"

"You forget. I am —"

"I know. A Sagoma." There was no way except to play her game.

"It means your mother was not lost in the Gulf, and that her brother and Tom's father and his Uncle Malvern were at her funeral. That's what it means."

"You weren't there long enough to see all that!"

"When you travel back in time, it is accomplished in *seconds*. Everyone knows that. Like dreams."

"And if Pasie had a funeral, I'd like to know why everyone thinks she was lost in the sea. And my diary got ruined!" I added pathetically.

"Your *mother's* diary. And it certainly wasn't my fault," she said callously, standing up.

The tomb had lost its scariness. It was just a dusty old place to get out of. It *was* Holly's fault the diary was ruined. Everything was her fault, all because she had to play her Sagoma game. She hadn't once mentioned the code. Sagoma, ha!

By the time we got home, the paint Pasie had used to hide the prayers had acted like glue and stuck all of the pages together. I had lost my mother all over again.

CHAPTER XIX

T OM!" I called in a stage whisper. I waited outside
his window, ready to run if anyone but Tom appeared.

"Tom!" I called a little louder.

"Boo!" he shouted in my ear.

"You scared me!" I said.

"How could that scare you?" he asked. "In broad
daylight?"

"You didn't have to poke me in the ribs and scream in
my ear! I thought you were inside."

"I was on my way inside. You sure scare easy!"

"I do not."

"So, you're brave. What did you want?"

"Never mind," I said haughtily.

"Oh, come on, Addie, can't you take a joke? You're such a girl! I was going to ask you to go out with me Halloween but you're so scared . . ."

"I like being a girl and I am not scared of anything!"

"I bet you're not! How would you like to go into the graveyard on Halloween night by yourself? You wouldn't do that, would you?"

"Ha, you wouldn't either!"

"Last Halloween I did, when I was a whole year younger."

"I go to the graveyard all the time. Holly and I were there yesterday."

"*Day.* I'm talking about Halloween *night. Alone.*"

"Okay. Alone. On Halloween night."

"You'll have to prove that you went all the way to your tomb!" he said, grinning. "You can bring back one of those big white flowers your Aunt Eveline always puts there for All Saints' — and I'll be waiting at the gate." He was so pleased he could hardly stand it.

"I'll do it," I said. "And I am leaving your premises now."

"What did you come over for?"

"None of your business!"

"Aw, come on, Addie! Why did you come?"

I relented. "Has your Uncle Malvern ever said anything about Pasie? Like being at her funeral, maybe?"

"How could he have been there when she didn't have one?"

"I just thought — I don't know. Did he ever go to Honduras? Or your father — did he go?"

"How would I know?"

"Well, I just think your uncle knows something."

"What do you care? It's not your business."

"It is too! Look at this, Tom." I produced the sodden diary and waited for his sympathy, my tears ready. "Just when I'd broken the code, too."

"*You* broke the code? Did you read the diary?"

"I didn't get a chance. It got rained on first."

"That's too bad," he said with a definite lack of enthusiasm.

"Don't cry," I said.

"I'll try not to."

"Thanks for nothing," I said, turning on my heel.

"Keep the change," he answered.

I marched straight home, my anger laced with self-pity. My two best friends — my only friends — had let me down. Sister Elizabeth Anne was one hundred percent correct — lay up your treasures in Heaven, she said, because you sure can't count on anyone down here. At least that's what she must have meant.

I was pondering these truths as I passed Aunt Eveline's room. Her door was ajar, and I looked inside and saw her sitting by the window, her back to me. She was bent over something. I didn't mean to sneak up on her, but I walked across the room and looked over her shoulder in time to see her paintbrush sweep upward in one movement, leaving a gnarled tree trunk in its wake. Quickly she dipped her brush into the paint again and swept it across the top of the paper, creating a darkening sky. I gasped as I recognized my mother's impressionistic style.

"Addie!" Aunt Eveline spun around, hugging the wet watercolor to her bosom. "What are you doing here?"

"You're ruining it!" I cried. "And it's beautiful! Don't smear it! You paint like my mother, Aunt Eveline! I thought you said — Aunt Eveline, how can you bear to do those dogs?"

"I don't mind the dogs, dear, and no one buys landscapes. In oil, yes, but not in watercolor."

"Aunt Eveline, the watercolor you gave me is yours! *You* did it!"

"Oh, no, dear! Your mother was the landscape painter of the family!"

"Aunt Eveline, it looks just like the painting you're doing now."

She let the smeared watercolor fall on her lap.

"Oh, Addie!" Tears formed in Aunt Eveline's eyes. "I wanted you to see something your mother had painted, dear. It was all lost. There wasn't anything yet. She was still developing, you know, and I only had sketches, exercises really. But she became a great artist in Honduras! And I wanted you to know that, dear. So when you liked my watercolor, why, I just said it was your mother's." Aunt Eveline looked at me wistfully. "Funny thing," she added, "I almost came to believe it was."

"Aunt Eveline, the watercolors my mother did are the ones in the attic, in the blue box."

"Oh, those. Those are only the exercises she did before she left, dear."

"Aunt Eveline, they are finished, worked-over watercolors. And they're bad."

Before she could answer, a new thought came to me. "Aunt Eveline, did you paint the portrait?"

"Why, yes, dear, I thought you knew."

"No, I didn't." I had never thought of who had done it. "You are the painter of the family, Aunt Eveline!" I said.

"Oh, no, dear! Your mother's watercolors that she painted in Honduras —"

"Did you ever see one, Aunt Eveline?"

"Well, she could never actually send one. The minute she finished a painting, someone snapped it up."

"Aunt Eveline, my mother didn't paint anything in Honduras."

"Addie! How can you say that? She wrote that the people down there, the wealthy planters, you know, practically fought over her paintings. Your mother was a wonderful painter! Wonderful!"

I put my fingers in my ears and shouted, "My mother was a paper doll!" and ran out of the room.

Aunt Eveline didn't mention the incident at dinner, but it hung between us, heavy as a wet sheet on a clothesline. I felt shy with her, and she seemed embarrassed and formal with me. Then, the next day, she was back to normal, as though nothing had happened. But things had shifted. Now I knew my mother had never been a real artist. I knew, too, that she had not been absolutely perfect and divinely happy. She seemed to need me; she seemed to need a friend.

I began to badger Aunt Eveline for art lessons. At first she resisted with the same old arguments about proper training, but she couldn't keep up the pretense of not being a "real artist," and her arguments couldn't stand up under my barrage.

"Aunt Eveline," I said one day when I came home from school, "please stop writing those notes and let's go to the park and paint." The afternoon was beautiful.

"These notes must be written, Adelaide. All of these people," she held out a long list of names, "came to Kate's funeral, and each must be thanked personally."

"Why should *you* thank them?" I said. "They came for Aunt Kate's sake, supposedly. It's her job."

"Addie," Aunt Eveline said coldly, "it goes without

saying that only one of the living can write thank-you notes."

"Maybe so," I snapped back. "But since Aunt Kate is now in Heaven, she can do better than notes, she can personally tell God just how good all those folks were to come to the funeral and eat Nini's sandwiches, and how they should be rewarded accordingly, and that beats anything you can do from down here!"

"Ad —" Aunt Eveline's shocked look collapsed into laughter. "Oh, Addie! How can I be angry with you? If ever you learn to paint as clearly as you think, you'll be an artist. I'll get my watercolors and paper. Fill a water jar in the kitchen, and we'll take the little rag rug in the upstairs hall to sit on."

"Okay! Okay, Aunt Eveline!"

"Addie?"

"I mean, Yes, indeed, Aunt Eveline!"

We had a marvelous afternoon. We sat by the lagoon and painted in the changing light.

"Look for the form, Addie," Aunt Eveline said over my shoulder. "Feel the roundness of that tree trunk, its strength, the turning that took years. Paint the slow growth. No, no, don't erase! Let it stand. Put it down true the first time!"

We didn't come home until the light was gone. A whole new world had opened up. We would paint every single afternoon. I'd be famous before I was out of high school.

"Oh, Addie, let's have an easy supper!" Aunt Eveline said, coming through the front door and throwing off the grey silk scarf she'd tied around her head. Soft curls framed her face. "I don't feel like cooking meat, rice, and a vegetable."

"Let's have tomato surprise!" I said. "I'll fix it."

Aunt Eveline sat down and watched as I toasted and buttered two slices of bread, and put first a slice of to-mato, then a hunk of yellow cheese, and a strip of bacon on each. Three minutes under the broiler and the bacon was curling over deliciously melting, golden cheese and hidden, ripe tomato. I poured two glasses of milk, and we brought our supper to the front porch. We sat in rockers, eating and laughing at George Burns and Gracie Allen on the radio. It had been an absolutely perfect day, the first of many to come, I thought.

But the next day, Aunt Eveline sat at her desk until she'd finished every note on her list, and no amount of pleading by me could budge her. When she was through the last one, she went into the kitchen and fixed us a huge dinner of pot roast, mashed potatoes, and snap beans. It wasn't even Nini's day off but she did it alone. I was painting upstairs. If I couldn't paint with Aunt Eveline, I'd paint alone in my room. It was like a disease; I couldn't stop. When I showed Aunt Eveline my work, she hardly looked. "Good, Addie. Splendid," she said, mashing the potatoes so hard she seemed to be trying to drive them through the pot. She was back to normal. But I knew there was another Aunt Eveline hiding behind the dog portraitist. And I thought I had it figured out why she couldn't just be herself.

CHAPTER XX

~~~~~~~~~~~~~~~

T HE REASON FOR Halloween," said Aunt Eveline, throwing her voice as though she were still in the classroom, "is, of course, All Saints' Day. Halloween is merely the *eve* of that important feast to honor the dead. And so, on Halloween morning, we will go to Saint Louis #2, tidy up the grave, and decorate it for All Saints' Day with these lovely chrysanthemums." Aunt Eveline produced five large, white flowers like the kind Homecoming Queens carry. "Addie, why are you looking so sullen?"

It was useless telling her. I was sure she didn't want to give me any more watercolor lessons because she was afraid of stealing my mother's place in my heart. Besides that, the diary had defeated me, and none of my friends liked me. I could have come up with a dozen more reasons for feeling mean, but I had enough, so I decided to state my philosophy about All Saints' Day.

"It's dumb to put flowers on the tomb for dead people. They don't know you're doing it, and if they do, they're supposed to be playing their harps in Heaven or something and don't care anyhow."

"*Addie!*"

"Well, it's true, isn't it? You really put flowers for all the other people who're putting flowers on their tombs so the others will say, 'My, my, look at those gorgeous chrysanthemums. I hope ours look that expensive!'"

"*Ah-de-la-eed!* Go to your room!" Aunt Eveline's voice shook and squeaked. I hadn't meant for her to get so excited.

Aunt Eveline followed me upstairs. By the time she got to my room she had control of herself.

"Addie," she said, "through tragic circumstances, your mother is not actually in the tomb with Uncle Ben and the others, but when you put flowers there you are honoring her. It has nothing to do with the living. You are telling her you love her, and she hears you."

"Aunt Eveline," I said trying to be truthful, but not wanting to risk her anger again, "I don't even remember my mother. How can I really love her?"

"Why, simply because she is your mother!"

"But I can't! You're much more like my real mother!"

This upset Aunt Eveline almost as much as my opinion of All Saints' Day customs.

"No, no!" she cried. "Oh, poor Pasie! You must love her, Addie! Maybe I haven't told you enough about how lovely she was."

"Yes, you have, Aunt Eveline! I know all that. All right, I'll put flowers on the tomb and I'll think of my mother. I love my mother."

"That's better, dear," she said, exhausted. "I know she'll be happy."

For the first time I realized what a strain I put on Aunt Eveline, and how seriously she took her obligation to raise me and keep my mother's memory alive. I remembered Aunt Toosie was worried about her. She did look tired. I promised myself not to give her any more trouble. Ever. I promised I would be the person she wanted me to be. I lectured myself all the way out to the front porch, where Sandra Lee was sitting.

"What are you going to be on Halloween?" Sandra Lee asked me.

"I haven't thought about it."

"I'm going to be the Angel Gabriel."

"The Angel Gabriel! That hasn't got anything to do with Halloween!"

"It has too. You can be anything you want on Halloween, and I have my costume from the Christmas play." Aunt Toosie had made Sandra Lee's costume, all white see-through tulle and golden gauze wings. "I heard Aunt Eveline say you were going to wear your Joseph costume."

"I am not! It's got a beard!" Aunt Eveline had made mine out of burlap sack and a mask Uncle Ben had worn in a Mardi Gras ball. She'd cut off the top part of the mask, leaving the beard and perpetually leering lips. It was a hideous costume and about as comfortable as a hair shirt. I marched into the house and up the stairs.

"Aunt Eveline!" I shouted. I went to her door and banged on it. "Aunt Eveline!"

144

The door opened and Aunt Eveline, very pale, rosary in hand, said quietly, "Addie, do not shout. If you wish to speak to me, come into my room so that you can speak in a normal tone."

"Aunt Eveline, I am not going to be Joseph on Halloween."

"It's the only costume you have! You make a splendid Joseph!"

"I don't want to make a splendid Joseph. I want to be pretty," I said desperately.

Aunt Eveline looked at me. "I thought the object of a Halloween costume was to disguise the real person."

"No, it isn't. It's to try to make them look better than they usually look. At least, that's what I want to do."

"I see," Aunt Eveline said thoughtfully.

"Oh, please, Aunt Eveline!"

"All right, then, Addie. I'll help you make another costume. What would you like to be, dear?"

"A Southern Belle. With hoopskirts."

"Addie! That's too complicated! We haven't time! I couldn't do that."

"We could use the portrait dress."

"The *portrait dress?* You want to wear your mother's beautiful dress? On Halloween? It's *much* too good. We can't consider it! Besides, there's no hoop in it."

"Please, Aunt Eveline! I'll make the hoop."

"Absolutely not! How can you possibly make a hoop?"

"I'll figure it out. With coat hangers! It's easy!"

She looked at me again and sighed. I had won.

"Oh, Addie! You would have to be *very, very* careful. You wouldn't want to put a spot on that lovely dress that belonged to your mother. We'd have to sew the hoop in very carefully."

"I'll get it!"

Aunt Eveline sighed again. "All right," she said wearily. "Here's the key."

She handed me the key with the blue ribbon. I rushed up the attic steps and tiptoed to the chest. I stopped. Pasie didn't want me to wear her dress. I told myself to stop imagining nonsense and unlocked the top. The dress was lying between layers of tissue paper. I lifted it out and pressed the soft silk against my cheek, smelling the perfume that clung to all of Pasie's things no matter how many mothballs Aunt Eveline threw around. I was going to wear the dress that had been too good to take to Belize!

JANE WHITMORE IN BELIZE

The ceiling fan hummed over my head as I lay on the bed and dreamed of home. I thought of the high, cool ceilings, the shuttered windows, and my canopied bed at Three Twenty Audubon Street.

Eveline's voice and Nini's drifted up from downstairs where they worked together moving chairs and arranging flowers for my party. I was going to put on the white dress Eveline had made for me when she painted my portrait. I would wear my gold heart around my neck. I started to get up, lifted my head from the pillow, and remembered: the dress was in the attic at Three Twenty, and it wasn't Eveline and Nini I heard, but Lola and Sussanah. They were coming down the road on their stupid burro from market where, no doubt, they'd bought corn and meat for tortillas, and their stew would smell up the whole house in a few minutes.

I cannot face another meal. The meat is goat. And — and, I don't want to look at George. I don't want to see his sad, heavy face across the table. When he pulls my chair out, if he touches me, I'll cry. I hate his being nice as though I were an invalid. I want Eveline, and, oh, God, I want Edmond! If only I could talk to him! Just to see him and tell him everything. He'd come if I wrote. If he understood how much I needed him. I could make him understand! Or, I wouldn't have to say exactly. I could pretend both George and I wanted him to visit us, as a friend, to see the interesting country. Yes, that's it! A visit from a friend.

CHAPTER XXI

WHEN AUNT EVELINE and I had finished constructing the hoop out of coat hangers, Aunt Eveline basted it in all around, making little comments the whole time like, "For heaven's sake, *be careful!*" When she had finished anchoring it securely to the skirt, I climbed in.

"We don't have to shorten the hem," Aunt Eveline said. "The hoop makes it just the right length." She looked in the mirror with me. "I remember dressing your mother in this dress," she said, tears in her eyes. "She tucked a gardenia in her hair and said, 'Do you think he'll like me, Eveline?' She meant your father, of course. I always think of your mother when I smell gardenias."

"There're still some in the yard! I'll wear one, too!"

Aunt Eveline didn't answer. She touched my black bangs hanging in my eyes and I thought she was comparing them unfavorably to Pasie's blond curls.

"You look like your mother," she said softly. "Darling Pasie!"

When I dressed Halloween evening, I pinned my bangs back with bobby pins and a gardenia over each ear so that, from the front at least, my hair looked long. The dress had a shape of its own; the lace collar made a low, round neckline with fullness in the right places, and it was possible to believe, since you couldn't say for sure what was under the hoop, that I had hips. Sandra Lee came in and gasped, "You look pretty!"

She hadn't mean to say it, but she didn't take it back after it slipped out. She gulped, flapped her gold wings, and added generously, "You really do."

"Thank you," I said. Of course, she looked gorgeous. "You look nice, too," I mumbled. It was the first time we'd ever said anything kind to each other.

Holly came as a Sagoma. She wore a length of striped cloth wrapped like a sarong and a dozen strings of Mardi Gras beads around her neck. Instead of flour on her face, she'd smeared real red clay, and in place of the scarf, she plaited her hair in a million small plaits showing the nice shape of her head. She looked African and authentic; she was too excited to remember she was mad at me.

"Now, girls," Aunt Eveline began, "I don't want you running around asking for candy at every door, like beggars." Aunt Eveline always missed the point. "Just walk around quietly and if anyone gives you candy, say thank you, and eat only a small amount and —"

Aunt Eveline was running on forever about Halloween etiquette when a sheeted figure crashed through the screen door, partly because that is the way Tom naturally goes through doors and partly because this time, another sheeted figure had stepped on Tom's sheet, twisting it so that the holes for his eyes were in back of his head.

I was about to tell him and Harold how unoriginal their costumes looked when Tom pulled the sheet off and said, "Addie?" in an unnatural voice. He was staring at me, and I decided it was a compliment.

"Stay in the neighborhood. *Be careful of the dress,*" Aunt Eveline continued. "Don't . . ."

Aunt Eveline didn't stop giving advice until we were out of earshot.

"We'll go to a few houses first," Tom announced, bossy as usual, but still staring at me. "That way you'll have something to eat if you get hungry in the graveyard all by yourself."

We only had to go to Aunt Toosie's, because she gave us so many oatmeal cookies, even Tom and Harold had enough.

"You don't have to go if you're scared," Tom said, relenting, but we were already waiting for the streetcar.

"So you can win," I answered. "I'm not scared."

When we arrived at Saint Louis #2 the gate was locked. I smiled wickedly at Tom. "So you went in the graveyard on Halloween night last year? How?"

"It was a little before absolute dark, I guess, but it was getting dark, and it was full of shadows and dark places. You don't have to keep the bet, Addie," he added magnanimously.

"I'm going in," I said. "You'll have to boost me."

"Don't go, Addie!" Holly was peering through the gate at the moonlit city of the dead. "Something's waiting for you! I see it!"

"Oh, go on in," said Sandra Lee. "We came all this way."

"I don't see anything," said Harold, "except, of course, some dead people and a few ghosts. Ha, ha."

"I'm not afraid," I answered, with as much nonchalance as I could muster. "Make a basket for my foot."

Tom and Harold wove their hands together. I hoisted the hoop out of the way, put one foot in the basket, and swung over the gate. As my feet touched the earth, the same thought occurred to five people at once.

"How are you going to get back?" the four on the outside chorused.

"I — I don't know!" I wailed.

"I'm coming, too," said Tom. "Make a basket."

"No! No, don't," I said. "Wait till I get back with the chrysanthemums." And, bravely turning my back on the gate, I started down the narrow aisle between the little houses where dead people slept.

Clouds racing over the moon made ghost shadows on the white tombs, and the wind whispered its way around corners, changing the ferns that grew from cracks in the tombs to tiny, nervous hands.

"Mother of God!" I said it out loud. The sharp shadow of my arm stabbed a stone angel. "I promise always to be good. I'll never aggravate Aunt Eveline again. I'll turn the other cheek to Sandra Lee. I'll —" I stopped. Everything looked different at night. I wasn't sure where the family tomb was. I saw a tomb where the entrance slab had fallen open; maybe the tomb Holly had gone into. I'd made so many turns, I wasn't even sure where the gate was, either. I turned around and walked back — I hoped. I'd admit defeat. I didn't care. My heart drowned out other sounds, and I'd run out of promises to offer up.

The moon came out from behind a cloud and lit some white chrysanthemums into tiny moons. They were decorating a more elaborate tomb-house than ours, one that had an iron grille fence forming a little yard in front. The chrysanthemums were in a vase on the tomb-house steps, behind the gate. Tom would never know the difference. I pushed at the gate and saw in the moonlight a small lock holding it closed. I hitched my skirt in the hoop again and put my foot on the gate handle. I jumped over the fence and grabbed one of the chrysanthemums. Footsteps — I heard footsteps! I knocked over the vase, and it fell on the stone steps with a crash that blotted out all of the noise in the world, leaving everlasting silence and — footsteps. Closer. I couldn't find a place to put my foot on that side of the fence. I was going to die of fright right there. I looked up and saw — oh, Lord! I saw Uncle Ben's ghost coming toward me! I could see his eye sockets and his mustache. I could see his lower jaw working. He was stretching out his arms toward me. I turned and threw myself over the opposite corner of the fence and tried to run. Something held me fast. I screamed and screamed and, in between screams, just before I fainted, I heard the ghost cry out in anguish, "Pasie!" Then, the nightmare wave washed over me, drowning out consciousness.

I came to, smelling water that stunk like flowers in a vase too long. I was propped up against the tomb, and Tom was sloshing chrysanthemum water in my face with the end of his sheet. "Addie! Wake up! Please wake up!"

"Ugh," I said. "Stop putting that smelly water on me!"

Something almost as frightening as the ghost was flying around at the back of my mind. I brought it forward and remembered hearing the sound of tearing silk. I looked down at an enormous slash in my mother's dress where an iron picket had gone through the skirt when my hoop caught on the fence. I had pulled so hard, I'd bent the hoop into an oval and one side of the dress was torn from waist to hem.

The ghost was sitting on some tomb steps a few feet away, his head in his hands. "Addie," he mumbled in shamed tones, "I thought you were Pasie! You looked just like her. *Just* like her . . ." His voice trailed off in a beery sigh.

"Uncle Malvern, what are you doing here?" asked Tom in disgust.

"Huh?" said Uncle Malvern.

"It's night, Uncle Malvern. What are you doing in the cemetery at night?"

"Same thing you're doing, boy — not much!" Uncle Malvern laughed happily at his joke.

Tom groaned, too humiliated to speak.

"Came for All Saints' Day," said Uncle Malvern. "To see the flowers."

"But it's nighttime! The cemetery's closed," Tom said.

"Wasn't when I came." Uncle Malvern chuckled at his second joke. "I — I fell asleep, I guess. Came at five," he added sheepishly and sighed more beer.

"Let's get out of here," Tom said sternly, pulling me up. "Come on," he added roughly to Uncle Malvern.

"Here, Uncle Malvern," I said, giving him my hand. "Let me help you up."

"Thank you, my dear. I can manage now." He rose with dignity.

We must have made a strange sight sauntering down the aisle of the moonlit cemetery, my arm through Uncle Malvern's, my other hand clutching the dress and lopsided hoop, which swung from side to side, banging three sets of knees. Tom's hand felt firm and good on my shoulder. I didn't even feel like pretending it belonged to Edmond. And even though I'd ruined my mother's dress, when I saw the Angel Gabriel flying around at the gate, flapping her wings at Harold and Holly, I was glad I had not gone as Joseph. The guard was there, too, and opened the gate.

"You folks is plumb crazy!" he said, recognizing Holly and me. "It's against the rules, me letting you out, and it's against the rules you getting in. I'll have to report you. Plumb crazy!"

When I got home, I crept upstairs, praying Aunt Eveline wouldn't hear me. I ripped the hoop out of the portrait dress and stuffed it behind my pillow. First thing in the morning, I'd ask Nini to mend it, and maybe Aunt Eveline would never notice if I put it back in the chest right away.

I crawled into bed, but both Jane Whitmore and sleep were far away. Instead I thought of Pasie. I guess it was wearing her dress, and Uncle Malvern thinking I was Pasie, that made her seem very near, a girl only a little older than me, someone I knew and could understand. And I remembered another white dress, a short, summer one. A scene so clear it could have been a memory came to me.

"George, she's too young to be without me. She needs me!"

"Pasie, if you leave, you leave without your child. Lola can take care of Addie. She can do anything you can do, and better."

"There's one thing I can do better than Lola, that *only* I can do. I can be her mother. Oh, George, don't be so cruel!"

"*I* cruel! You are cruel, Pasie. You are leaving us!"

"No, George, I am only leaving *you*. I want my child."

"Pasie, you don't have to leave. Even now. Stay. We can all be together. Please. Please, Pasie!"

"You don't understand, George. The point is I can't stay. Try to understand that."

"I don't understand it. Every marriage has its ups and downs. We just have to weather the storm. I, for one, am ready to forget and forgive."

"George, it is not something you've done, or anything I've done. It's the way we are." She paused and then said slowly, without emotion, "I loathe you."

I was there, a small child running after her. Strong hands dragged me back. I called her until my throat ached, long after her thin, white-clad figure had disappeared into the banana trees. The man's arms held me close. I struggled, bit, and kicked, crying for my mother. I screamed myself hoarse, locked in unyielding arms.

"Addie!"

A pebble hit the screen. Then another, and another.

"Tom?" I struggled out of the scene, still clear and hard against a tropical sky.

"Are you awake?" Tom was under my window.

"I can't stop thinking about them!" I slid the screen up and leaned out of my window, glad Tom had come back and I could stop living that scene — a dream or a memory — it made no difference to the misery I felt.

"Who can't you stop thinking about?"

"Pasie, my mother, I mean, and my father. Where's Uncle Malvern?"

"I got him to bed. Come on down."

I didn't have a shortcut out of my window like Tom's and this house told secrets in squeaks and strange noises. I took the back stairs, creaking all the way. Aunt Eveline locked the back door at night, but left the key in the lock. I turned it, holding my breath. It groaned, practically calling Aunt Eveline. But the house remained absolutely quiet.

"Addie!" Tom was standing on the back porch. "You look like a ghost in that nightgown."

"That was a real Halloween, wasn't it?"

"Uncle Malvern is a fool. I hate him."

"Don't hate him. He's sad. He was young like us once. And he hoped for good things. He just never could make them happen. That's sad."

"I know something. I came to tell you."

"What?"

"I lied to you. I broke the code, too."

"*You did?* How?"

"With a word just three letters long repeated over and over. Like you did."

"What word?"

"I can't say."

"What do you mean, you can't say? Did you read the diary?"

"Part."

"Part! What did it say?"

"It was too personal. I felt funny reading it."

"But what did she *say?* What was personal?"

"It was about this guy, that's all. Mush. It was dumb. I didn't think you'd want to see it."

"But *you* saw it."

"I saw enough."

"Who was the guy? You mean she liked this man?"

"Yeah."

"Not my father?"

"No."

"Well, who?"

"Aw, Addie! Some guy. I don't know *who*. And Fifi. She misses Fifi almost as much as this man."

"Oh, poor Pasie! I wish I had read it!"

"It isn't your business."

"What do you mean 'isn't my business'? It was *my* diary."

"No, it was your mother's. *Her* secrets." He looked straight at me. "You shouldn't know other people's secret thoughts."

"I only wanted to know because she was my mother."

"That doesn't entitle you to her secrets." I didn't answer. He got up and added, "You wouldn't have known her secret thoughts if she'd lived. Any more than you know your Aunt Eveline's. Or mine, Addie."

"It was mean and contemptible of you not to tell me in the beginning."

"I'm sorry, Addie," he said, going down the steps. "I just wanted you to know I'd lied. See you."

"It's the lowest thing I ever heard of!" I said, getting madder the more I thought about it. Tom was out of sight, into the dark night.

I had a strong feeling he was still lying to me. Why hadn't he told me the word he'd seen repeated? I had an idea it was a name, a name we both knew. I remembered the three numbers I'd seen together just before I realized that four of them meant Fifi. They were 1, 15, and 26.

CHAPTER XXII

I STOOD AT THE DOOR to Uncle Malvern's room. I felt
foolish. I'd imagined the whole thing. He'd think I
was crazy.

"Uncle Malvern," I called timidly. "Aunt Eveline
baked some cookies for Aunt Mable."

No answer.

"Uncle Malvern," I said loudly. "I have cookies.
From Aunt Eveline!"

The door opened, blowing the sour smell of beer at
me. Uncle Malvern stood against the background of his
perpetual motion machine, a mass of wheels and chains
looming still as a tombstone.

"How nice, my dear," he said. "They look absolutely

yummy." Uncle Malvern was staring at me absentmind-
edly, as though he were trying to place me.

"Tell me about my mother!" I blurted.

"Your mother!"

I swallowed. "Did you love her? Did you love Pasie?"

"Pasie!" He gasped, recovered, and said, "Pasie. We
all loved her." His voice caught. "Yes, we all loved her."

"I mean, were you *in* love with her?" I could hardly
believe the words I was saying were mine.

"A lovely girl," he mumbled. "I used to look at her
when Eveline was painting the portrait. I thought she
was the most beautiful girl I'd ever seen." He sighed.

"Aunt Toosie says she was selfish," I said. "She says
Pasie took George away from Eveline. Aunt Toosie says
my father really loved Aunt Eveline, and I think Pasie
really loved you."

Uncle Malvern looked so startled I wished I could
take the words back.

"Brother and sister," he said in a rush. "We loved
each other like brother and sister. Poor Pasie!"

"Poor Eveline, it seems to me!" I said rudely.

"My dear, you're too young to understand."

"I'm not too young! I want to know."

"Yes, yes, of course you do. Of course you do! But
she was lovely, and we did all love her. If Toosie thought
her selfish, well, she was human. All the more beautiful
because of it." He sighed, and his watery blue eyes swam
more than ever.

I was afraid to breathe for fear he'd stop talking.

"You see, Pasie and I — we were good friends all of
our lives, like brother and sister. It wasn't George's fault,
but he didn't understand her. He was much older, and
he didn't realize how young and delicate she was — her

artistic temperament, you know. She became terribly thin in the climate out there — a wraith — and she didn't want to bother him because he had so much on his mind."

Uncle Malvern paused so long, I thought he'd forgotten he was talking to me.

"Pasie wasn't well, then?" I prompted.

"Yes! Yes, that was it! Of course! She wasn't herself, so thin and homesick."

Another pause.

"She missed Three Twenty Audubon Street?"

"Yes, Three Twenty and her little dog. When I visited, I found her terribly homesick. Eveline had spoiled her, you know."

"When did you visit her?" I asked, and held my breath for his answer.

"It was just before the hurricane." He stopped, a remembering look on his face. He had forgotten I was there. "Pasie asked me, begged me really, to bring her home. Of course, I couldn't do that!" Uncle Malvern stopped as though he had settled something with himself.

"And then, Uncle Malvern? Then what?"

"She was a trifle hardheaded, Pasie was. And, well, she left your father — and you — and went to the beach cottage."

"Alone?"

"Yes, all by herself."

"And then?"

"Then, the hurricane came, and the tidal wave." Uncle Malvern shuddered. "We were safe in your house, high in the hills, but Pasie — if *only* she hadn't left . . ."

"You mean we weren't all swept into the sea?"

"Oh, no! We were high in the hills!"

High and dry. We had been safe! The whole time!

My father hadn't saved me because I'd never even been in the water! My nightmare had nothing to do with me — only my mother.

"Was my mother — lost?" I couldn't say the word *drowned*.

"Not exactly."

"She wasn't lost in the Gulf?"

"Drowned, but not lost."

"But everyone told me — Uncle Malvern, what happened to her?"

"I found her afterward." Tears were rolling down his cheeks. "I brought her home at last."

"Home? Here?" I was crying, too. Each thing he said was a small explosion in my head. I'd said too much. Uncle Malvern suddenly seemed to know he wasn't talking to himself.

"Well, uh, well, yes, that is . . ."

"Is she buried in Saint Louis #2?" I asked.

He nodded his head like a small boy admitting he'd done something wrong. "Promise you won't tell Eveline and Toosie?" he pleaded.

"But why don't they know?" I asked.

"Oh, we *couldn't* tell the girls! It would have killed Eveline to know that Pasie had left George — and you. That things hadn't worked out between George and Pasie."

"But why did you bring her home? Why didn't my father bring her home? After she died?" Uncle Malvern looked confused. "Why didn't George bring Pasie home?" I asked.

"Oh, he wouldn't have done that! George was a good man, but after Pasie left him, he simply acted as though she had never existed. She was a pariah to him, as the Indians say — an outcast not to be spoken of. So, in the

161

end, I had to bring her home. No, we never could have told the girls," he repeated. "Pariah," he mumbled, blurring the word.

In the fading light of his bedroom, Uncle Malvern reminded me of someone. Under the soft layer of flesh, sliding into jowls, I saw a cleft chin; beneath the puffy, vein-lined nose, the bones formed a short straight line; the watery, bloodshot eyes were faded blue; the mustache drooped into a delicately shaped mouth. Under the mask worn by Uncle Malvern was Edmond Hilary de St. Denis! It was like a firecracker that only takes a second to go off, but my whole secret life lay in pieces at my feet. I had ripped off Uncle Malvern's mask and seen Edmond. But to Pasie, Malvern must have remained desirable, and maddeningly unattainable until the end.

"Thank you for telling me all of that, Uncle Malvern," I said. But he was half asleep and smiled foolishly. "Good-bye, Uncle Malvern," I said. "Good-bye, Edmond," I whispered.

I went home shaken by my mother's unhappiness. I pitied my father, but I didn't understand how anyone could have been so cruel, not caring about Aunt Eveline, and then not understanding or ever forgiving my mother. I crawled into bed as unhappy as if it had all happened to me instead of to my mother. Then, when I tried to become Jane Whitmore, she became Pasie in a scene just before the hurricane.

"Malvern, bring me home! I can't stand this place!"

"But, my dear, you are married to George! He is your husband. It's his place to bring you home. He'll bring you home if he understands how you feel."

"No, he won't. He'll never understand. When I try to tell him, he pats my hands as though I were a child and says, 'You'll get used to it, Aspasie. It always takes time.' And then, he looks at me with those sad, droopy eyes. Did you ever notice that he looks like an old cocker spaniel?"

"Pasie!"

"Even his mustache droops — like ears."

"Now, Pasie, he is your husband!"

"I don't like him!"

"Pasie! Don't say that. Don't think it."

"I hate him!"

"All right, all right, dear. We'll write Eveline."

"We'll *go!*"

"But Eveline — "

"It's not Eveline's business! Besides, she'd make me stay. She doesn't believe in quitting. 'Finish what you start' is her motto. I don't have to go home to Three Twenty, you know. I could go to New York. Nini could send Fifi. If you take me —"

"I? I can't take you, Pasie! What would people say?"

"I don't care what people would say! Oh, Mal, don't you understand me after all these years?"

"Yes, yes, of course, I do, my dear. But first we must write Eveline. Telegraph, if you prefer. You just can't . . ."

I saw him, finally. Why had it taken me so long? His cleft chin wasn't a sign of strength. It drew attention away from his weak mouth. His straight eyebrows met over watery blue eyes. He wouldn't help me because he couldn't. There was no one, not even myself. I threw myself on the bed in complete despair. Malvern sat on the edge, stroking my hand and dabbing at my tears.

"Oh, Pasie! Oh, my dear!" he murmured. Finally I stopped sobbing and fell asleep. When I awoke, I was alone. The wind had grown strong and had a voice I'd never heard before.

That was the last Jane Whitmore scene I ever had, and it was so vivid that after I went to sleep, I dreamed the hurricane nightmare. But this time, instead of being inside the wave, I was standing on a cliff watching Pasie at the beach cottage in Honduras. She was alone and had been crying, but now she stopped to listen to the wind. The wind howled at gale force, bending the trees down parallel to the ground. On the horizon, a dark curtain rose and moved toward land, carrying rain so opaque that Pasie did not see the great wave until it hit the cottage, tumbling it like paper. Pasie, who had turned into a paper doll, lay on the crest of the wave as it carried her gently to the foot of the cliff. Then the wave receded and left her lying there, golden curls and seaweed framing her white face.

She lay like Sleeping Beauty until the Prince came. He was riding a burro and looked dumpy, with a skimpy mustache, and thinning hair slicked down under his golden crown. He kissed Pasie and she woke up, three-dimensional again. She returned his kiss, transforming him into Edmond Hilary de St. Denis, handsome and strong. Together, they mounted the burro, which became a great white horse with a flowing mane and took them galloping through the banana trees toward the sea. Everything was beautiful in my dream, except that they forgot Pasie's white silk scarf and it hung, water-stained, on a tree blown leafless by the wind.

CHAPTER XXIII

I GULPED DOWN my prunes, gagging only once, and brought the plate to the kitchen.

"Where's Holly?" I asked Nini. I had to tell Holly that she was right about Uncle Malvern.

"Gone," Nini turned red eyes to me. "Gone to Chicago."

"But I have to tell her something! And she didn't even say good-bye!"

"I'm sorry about that, Addie. I'm truly sorry. She had to leave in a hurry. Her mama needed her — a new baby and a new daddy. I bet Holly is sorry she didn't say good-bye. It doesn't do for a person to go away without saying good-bye."

"She was my best friend," I whined.

"Is, Addie, is. The heart won't change. She'll be back come the summer. You'll see. Maybe back for good! I'm hoping . . . if Sarah . . ."

By summer, I'd be thirteen and Holly fourteen. Too old to be scared in the attic or even in the graveyard. Too old for anything fun. She'd never known she was my best friend. I'd never known it either.

"Holly has to get used to a new daddy," said Nini.

"Maybe he'll be nice," I answered without really thinking about it.

"Maybe." Nini slowed down polishing the silver. "He's got his family. Six children he's bringing for my Sarah to mind, and she's got four herself. All younger than Holly." Nini looked at me.

"I could write her," I said, ashamed I had not thought about Holly's problems or what her life was like at home in Chicago. It was a good thing she had her Sagoma gifts to help her.

Nini smiled. "Holly'd like for you to write," she said.

"I could tell her about Jane Whit — about Sandra Lee and me."

"Do that, Addie. You write her. Just tell her all that's happening here. How you and Sandra Lee are going to dancing school and catechism and all, and how Miss Eveline and Miss Toosie are looking so well. And how I'm waiting for the summer and hoping it'll be for good. Tell her I'm waiting."

"I'll write this minute, Nini. I'll bet she's forgotten she ever was mad at me."

"Good, honey, good. She'll like that." Nini was rubbing the pitcher so hard she'd soon be down to the brass. "Tell her all what you're doing. And tell her I'm waiting for summer."

I wrote. I was very humble and understanding. I forgave her, I said, for not saying good-bye. I understood her problems, I said, and she had my deepest sympathy. I told her I needed her Sagoma gifts and hoped she'd help me again in the summer. I mailed the letter, feeling virtuous, forgiving, understanding, mature, and full of wisdom. I hadn't felt so good since my last Confession.

I went over to Tom's house and told him about Holly leaving without saying good-bye and about the beautiful letter I'd written. I told him that one should not turn inward and become self-centered, that one should see another's needs. I told him that friendship is sacred and must be guarded jealously to keep the embers glowing.

I stood there expectantly, and Tom said, "Whew! I hope you don't write any mush like that to me."

"Don't worry!" I answered. "I wouldn't write you a letter if — if —" I couldn't think of anything. "And anyhow, you're here."

"I'm going away to school."

"You are! Oh, Tom. Where?" I forgot I was mad at him.

"A school in North Carolina. The boys work there. They do all of the chores, even help when there's a building to put up."

I would be all alone. Stuck at Three Twenty Audubon Street. Without any friends.

"But why, Tom? Do you want to leave?"

"Yes," he said. "And my mother thinks that since I have no father, I should grow up around boys and men more."

"Oh."

"I'll miss you, Addie."

"I'll —" I burst into tears.

"It's not till after Christmas, Addie. And I'll be home in the summer. It's not as though I were really leaving home. But, well, there's Uncle Malvern, and — I want to get away."

"I understand," I whimpered. "It's just that first Holly and now you, and that leaves just me — and Sandra Lee."

"You'll have Pumpkin! And listen, Addie, Sandra Lee's not so bad. You're pretty hard on her, you know."

"Me? Hard on *her?*"

"Well, aren't you?"

It was true I was always careful to say something mean as soon as I saw her, but that was just to make sure she didn't beat me to it.

"She doesn't know you," Tom went on. "You never give her a chance. You're so stuck-up."

"Me? Stuck-up? *Me?*"

"I bet Sandra Lee and Harold think so. You never talk to them."

"They don't talk to me!"

"But if they really knew you . . . When you smile . . . You could make friends."

I smiled through my tears and Tom laughed at me. "Not like that. You have to dry your eyes and blow your nose first." He gave me his handkerchief. I looked at it carefully and decided to use the hem of my dress.

"Tom," I said, trying out the smile again. "What was the word you used to break the code? The one with three letters repeated over and over. It wasn't Mal, was it? Short for Malvern?"

"How did you know?"

"I asked him if he'd loved her. I thought so because of how he said her name that night in the cemetery."

"Yeah. It was his name. How could she ever have liked *him?*"

"He used to be good-looking."

"That's hard to believe. But even so, I'll bet he was always — always *just* like he is now."

I didn't answer. I knew Tom had lied because he was so ashamed of Uncle Malvern, he didn't want to tell me my mother had liked him.

"Tom," I said, "you ought to *try* to like your Uncle Malvern. At least feel sorry for him, don't you think?"

"That's it, Addie!" Tom touched my mouth. "That's the smile I mean! When you smile like that you'll make friends!"

When I got home, I went straight to the mirror and smiled. I looked so fake and dumb, I laughed out loud, and caught the reflection of someone I didn't mind. I thought of what Holly had said, that if you believe you are someone, you are. Something like that she'd said. Maybe I was the girl I'd seen for a second in the mirror. I smiled at myself again, and Aunt Eveline, walking in unannounced as usual, caught me.

She politely pretended she hadn't seen and said, "I have to go downtown tomorrow. I was wondering if you'd care to look for a new dress to wear to dancing school? Miss Rush told me she saw one in Holmes's window that made her think of you."

The next morning, we were downtown when the stores opened. The dress was absolutely perfect — all white batiste, trimmed at the neck and sleeves with a pale blue ribbon running through eyelet lace. I loved it and said so.

"One loves people, adores God, and *likes* things," Aunt Eveline said, and commanded the saleslady to get the dress out of the window. Aunt Eveline felt the material, examined the lace, the stitches, the seams, and — the price tag. It read $16. Aunt Eveline said, "Thank you very much," to the saleslady, and with great dignity, on

her part, at least, we left. We went to the pattern depart-
ment, studied the pattern books, bought two patterns to
combine, one for the top and the other for the skirt. We
bought three yards of white batiste, two of eyelet lace
and blue ribbon, and returned home. We had spent $8.35,
including carfare.

I helped Aunt Eveline cut out the dress on the dining
room table, and after lunch we basted it and went next
door, where Aunt Eveline sat down at Aunt Toosie's sewing machine.

"Aunt Eveline," I said, as she began to take out pins
and pull threads. "I found out something."

"Hmm?"

"My mother is buried in Saint Louis #2."

Aunt Eveline opened her mouth and the straight pins
she'd been holding there fell, thank goodness, on the
floor and not down her throat. The color drained from
her face, but I continued.

"I found her gold heart in Saint Louis #2. Uncle Malvern told me everything. He and Uncle Ben buried her
there secretly because they didn't want to upset you. It's
true. Nini knows too. I thought you ought to know."

"All right, Addie," Aunt Eveline was in control of
herself and I had her full attention. "Let's have the
whole story."

I gave her the whole story. All of it that I knew, em-
bellished with the parts I'd filled in for myself. When I
was finished (her eyes had never left my face) I expected
her to rejoice. Her dearest wish had come true: darling
Pasie was buried in Saint Louis #2. Instead, she surprised me.

"You've grown up!" she said in amazement. And then,
anxiously, "Addie, dear, are you upset about all of this?"

"Oh, no, Aunt Eveline. I like knowing about my mother. I feel as though I know her now, and — I like her." I did not add: she seems more like a sister than a mother, and you, Aunt Eveline, seem like the mother of both of us.

Aunt Eveline smiled and sighed. She looked very tired. "You've grown up," she repeated.

I opened my mouth to say something nice, like "You've changed, too," but that didn't sound right and words wouldn't come.

She bent to pick up the pins. "Help me pick these up, Addie. I want to finish the seams and hem the skirt so that you'll have the dress for tonight." Then, she said the most amazing thing of all. "If only I hadn't meddled. If only I had just let things happen for once, I would have been the wife George wanted, and he would have been a different man."

I started to reply but couldn't think of a word to say, and anyhow, Aunt Eveline's foot was working the pedal so fast, she wouldn't have heard.

The dress was ready in plenty of time. Aunt Eveline and I surveyed it and congratulated ourselves on having duplicated the store dress exactly.

"Addie," Aunt Eveline said when I dressed for dancing school, "why don't you wear the locket?"

"The locket?"

"Your mother's gold heart. Bring it to me."

I ran to my room and brought it back in record time.

Aunt Eveline received the heart as though it were the Holy Grail. She took a straight pin and touched a tiny hole right at the top. It sprang open into a locket, with the picture of a very small girl inside. I saw her black straight bangs before tears blinded me.

"Now you know who was in her heart, Addie," Aunt Eveline said.

My dress was by far the prettiest one at dancing school; at least I thought so, and as Sandra Lee and Harold glided by, Sandra Lee said over his shoulder, "That's a pretty dress, Addie," which is really not as good as "You look pretty, Addie."

Still, it was something, so I swallowed twice, remembered what Tom had said about being hard on Sandra Lee, gave a fleeting thought to the Baltimore Catechism, and blurted, "You look really cute, Sandra Lee! But then, you always do!"

Sandra Lee's mouth fell open and she tripped over Harold's foot, but she recovered enough to say, "Gee, thanks, Addie!"

Tom danced with me twice all the way to the end of both dances. Even Harold danced with me once, which turned out to be enough because he was wearing his hair tonic that made me long for Uncle Ben's gas mask. I didn't have to hide in the back for the contest, because, although Tom escaped and went home ahead of time and I didn't have a partner, I had danced enough to feel generous, so I stood around talking to Denise and Elizabeth and practicing my new smile on the chaperones.

"Well, Addie," Miss Rush said at the end of dancing school, "you were the belle of the ball!"

"The dress," I murmured, wondering why grown-ups say stupid things.

"No, my dear," she said, terribly pleased with herself. "Just Addie, undisguised by Lily Dior."

"Thank you, Miss Rush," I said politely, and got away as quickly as possible. I ended up walking home with Harold and Sandra Lee, surprised at how much nicer they seemed. Maybe Tom was right about the way I treated Sandra Lee.

Tom *was* right about Sandra Lee. The day after he left for North Carolina, Sandra Lee just up and said, "I have decided that I owe more to my very own blood cousin than to the members of the Secret Society. Here are two of my extra Ovaltine tops!"

It took two weeks for my badge to come, but after that I was a spy! No longer an Outsider! I could decode the secret message, and I'd never even taken a sip of Ovaltine.

Life was tolerable, until one afternoon at the end of April.

"Aunt Eveline, I'm home!" I hollered from the foot of the stairs, wondering why she wasn't bustling around. It was our afternoon to go to the park, but it was cold and cloudy. I thought that maybe we could paint a still life inside. I ran up the stairs, and just before I burst into her room, I heard her cough.

"Aunt Eveline . . ."

She was lying in bed, saying her rosary. Her hair was loose, and from the doorway she looked like a young girl, but when I went over to her bedside, I saw she looked old — *really* old! Like Aunt Kate when she was preparing for the next life. I wanted to yell, "Get up, Aunt Eveline, it's too soon to prepare!" Instead, I mumbled something about painting. I felt weak in the knees and sick in the stomach.

"Oh, Addie," Aunt Eveline said in a funny voice after she'd answered, yes, dear, a still life, now nice. "Addie, I wanted to ask a favor of you."

"Hunh?" I couldn't concentrate.

"Addie."

"I mean, what is it, Aunt Eveline?"

"Well, you've heard of double weddings, dear, and this would be — something like that. He's bound to be gone now, of course."

"*Who,* Aunt Eveline?"

"Ben. So I can go to Saint Louis #2. And if, at the same time, we bring Katie — space would hardly be a problem for her at this point — dust to dust, you know — why, with Pasie there, we'd all be together!"

Aunt Eveline was talking about dying! *Herself!* Aunt Eveline meant Aunt Kate was a little pile of dust now, easy to move. She was talking about mass burial at Saint Louis #2!

"Would you ask Toosie to do this for me?"

"Aunt Eveline! You can't *die!* Oh, please Aunt Eveline!"

"Now, Addie, everyone has to pass on, and when the Lord calls, if one hasn't excellent reasons for delay, one should answer, 'Yes, Lord, I am ready!' and now that I see you have grown up so much, Addie, if I could just solve this nagging problem of Kate! *Stuck* out there! Miles away! In a *hole* in the ground! If I could just know Kate was settled in — oh, Addie — I'm tired. I see no reason for keeping the Lord waiting."

"No, Aunt Eveline!" I yelled. *"Please!"*

"Addie, dear, won't you do this for me?"

She meant it.

"Please, Addie?"

"Yes, I'll do *anything* you say. And I'll never aggravate you again! But listen, Aunt Eveline, you can't —"

"Thank you, dear!" Aunt Eveline chatted on about seeing to it Toosie didn't do anything bohemian, and about what she wanted to wear for the occasion, "the

grey scarf, dear, in my top drawer, dear, the one your father gave me, will be quite appropriate with Uncle Ben's Navy League pin, but not, please, that lavender polka-dotted thing, I've always hated it."

I sat there in shock. There were a million things I wanted to say, like, "I can't go on without you, Aunt Eveline!" but that sounded melodramatic even though it was true. What would I do without her? I couldn't say any of it.

Aunt Eveline, between coughs, hadn't stopped talking. "And, now, dear, you must remember not to go to that place either!"

"What place, Aunt Eveline?" I asked, numb.

"Metairie Cemetery!" she said emphatically. "Just be careful and *remember:* it's merely a question of timing!"

CHAPTER XXIV

～～～～～～～～～

IT WAS JUST as Aunt Eveline wanted, including the Aunt Kate part. They were all together now, Eveline, Kate, and Pasie, part of the crowd at Saint Louis #2 waiting for the Last Day. All we could do was bring flowers to the cemetery and remind the Lord not to call us unless there was a vacancy.

My only trouble was tears. I couldn't stop crying. I had lost the person I loved best. Sandra Lee cried too, and, for once, she didn't bother to toss her curls or seem to care that her eyes were puffy and her nose so swollen and red, it wouldn't have twitched if she'd tried.

I wanted to turn back the clock and prove to Aunt Eveline that I understood the loving-kindness she'd always shown me — and my mother. But besides gratitude for all of that, I desperately wanted her to know I loved her because — well, because she was Aunt Eveline.

When we knelt in Saint Louis #2, I prayed: Please, God, let her know all of that! And give unto her a good seat in Heaven, next to Pasie, and near a window where she can hear when I call!

Nini had come to live at our house during the short time Aunt Eveline was sick, but when the funeral was over, she announced that since Holly was coming for good, she was going to retire and keep house for Holly while she got her education.

"I'll see you, now, Addie, make no mistake! And I'll help you all when I can, but, just think, Holly'll be here all the time! That girl is some smart! She . . ." The only way to stop Nini was to quit listening.

If ever I had wanted to be Jane Whitmore, it was the day after the funeral. I lay in bed that last morning at Three Twenty and shut my eyes tight.

"Add-dee! Ah-de-lah-eed, dear!" Aunt Toosie's voice bounced cheerfully up the steps.

It wouldn't work. I opened my eyes.

"Addie!" Aunt Toosie was coming down the hall. "Come get your breakfast, dear!" The door opened. "Addie, come, dear. Your room is ready too, dear. Right next to Sandra Lee's. And Uncle Henry will move your bed over today. Come, dear."

I got out of bed, pulled my nightgown over my head and stepped first into my underpants, then into my cotton plaid with the smocked front. Jane Whitmore would never have stepped into a dress; she would have slipped into a dress. She would have . . .

I went next door. I walked by way of the sidewalk

instead of through the cherry laurel hedge. My place was set between Uncle Henry and Sandra Lee. They looked at me as I stood in the doorway. Slowly, in a courtly fashion, Uncle Henry rose, dabbing his mouth with his napkin.

"Sit here, Addie." Sandra Lee touched the chair next to her.

The kitchen smelled of bacon and buttered toast and the slightly burnt starch in Aunt Toosie's red and white checked cloth. Uncle Henry pulled the chair out for me. Aunt Toosie had cooked crisp bacon and fluffy scrambled eggs. No prunes. No wrinkled prunes floating in brown juice. No ghastly, slimy things to get down. No Aunt Eveline to make me do it. I put my hands over my face and sobbed. Aunt Toosie's arms came around me and she said, "It'll be all right, Addie, dear! Just cry. Cry every single tear out, and it'll be all right."

The next week someone bought Three Twenty Audubon Street, and "modernized" it. They enclosed the front screen porch and painted the old house a tacky yellow with fake white shutters on the front. They draped the windows in chintz and organdy. It was as though the poor old house, in a fit of envy, was trying to look like its young neighbor full of ruffles. I was embarrassed for Three Twenty. By the time the work was complete, at least I could take comfort knowing Holly and Tom would soon be home.

Then one morning in June, I heard Pumpkin barking wildly. "Addie! Addie!" Tom hollered as he crashed through Aunt Toosie's kitchen door. "You've got to come see it!"

"See what?" I hollered back from upstairs, thinking how very little that young man had changed since Christmas, whereas I had grown serene and mature and could no longer be mistaken for a boy.

"Wait till you see it!" he said when I stood next to him. Tom seemed to be looking down at me from much farther up than before. His cheekbones were different and so were his eyebrows. Paler freckles covered a straight, short nose, and his smile was . . . I liked his smile.

"Hi," I said shyly.

"Come on," he said. I was very conscious of his hand pulling mine.

It was a good thing I'd grown up since Christmas and learned serenity and tolerance, because he never stopped talking the whole way to his house. I didn't hear exactly what he was saying, because I was intent on a squeak in every tenth word or so, as though he needed oiling.

"There!" he said, finally throwing open Uncle Malvern's door. Uncle Malvern was seated on top of his invention, which was much more complicated than before, and now grew from the floor almost to the ceiling. It was turned on and gave the impression of forward motion, because the head of Tom's old rocking horse was stuck at one end and the tail at the other.

"It's a modern Trojan horse!" cried Uncle Malvern from near the ceiling.

"It's not so bad, is it?" Tom whispered to me. "Poor guy! Say something nice to him."

"It's very nice, Uncle Malvern," I said.

"You bet!" Uncle Malvern replied. "Giddy yap!"

"Addie," Tom said, suddenly and without a squeak, "you're so pretty! But then, you always were."

"Oh," I said. "Uh. Um."

It wasn't until after I went to bed that night that I

thought up an answer: "It is the inner, spiritual self, Tom, that has grown serene and lovely, shining through. It is that you perceive."

"It is all of you, inside and out!" Tom said, his voice breaking with emotion.

I blushed becomingly and answered, "I am more than pleased, Tom, to glimpse in you, too, signs of maturation, such as your more compassionate treatment of your uncle, and — and, I like what your mouth does when you smile."

It was just as well I hadn't said it; best to let him see for himself, rather than tell him, how modest and mature I'd become.

MS READ-a-thon—
a simple way to start
youngsters reading

Boys and girls between 6 and 14 can join the MS READ-a-thon and help find a cure for Multiple Sclerosis by reading books. And they get two rewards — the enjoyment of reading, and the great feeling that comes from helping others.

Parents and educators: For complete information call your local MS chapter. Or mail the coupon below.

Kids can help, too!

Mail to:
National Multiple Sclerosis Society
205 East 42nd Street
New York, N.Y. 10017
I would like more information about the MS READ-a-thon and how it can work in my area.

Name_____
(please print)
Address_____
City_____ State_____ Zip_____
Organization_____

1—80

A PUBLIC SERVICE MESSAGE FROM DELL PUBLISHING CO., INC.